A
STAR TREK NOVEL
BY JAMES BLISH

SPOCK
MUST DIE!

BANTAM PATHFINDER EDITIONS
TORONTO / NEW YORK / LONDON

A NATIONAL GENERAL COMPANY

$$RLI: \frac{VLM\ 10.0}{IL\ 9\text{-}12}$$

SPOCK MUST DIE!

A Bantam Book / published February 1970

2nd printing ...... March 1970   4th printing ..... October 1971
3rd printing ... September 1970   5th printing .... February 1972
6th printing .... May 1972
Bantam Pathfinder edition published August 1972
8th printing ...... October 1972
9th printing

Bantam Books are published by Bantam Books, Inc., a National
General company. Its trade-mark, consisting of the words "Bantam
Books" and the portrayal of a bantam, is registered in the United
States Patent Office and in other countries. Marca Registrada.
Bantam Books, Inc., 666 Fifth Avenue, New York, N.Y. 10019.

PRINTED IN THE UNITED STATES OF AMERICA

To
Kay Anderson

CONTENTS

Author's Note

Unlike the preceding three STAR TREK books, this one is not a set of adaptations of scripts which have already been shown on television, but an original novel built around the characters and background of the TV series conceived by Gene Roddenberry. I am grateful to the many fans of the show who asked me to tackle such a project, and to Bantam Books and Paramount Television for agreeing to it.

And who knows—it might make a television episode, or several, some day. Although the American network (bemused, as usual, by a rating service of highly dubious statistical validity) has canceled the series, it began to run in Great Britain in mid-June 1969, and the first set of adaptations was published concurrently in London by Corgi Books. If the show is given a new lease on life through the popularity of British reruns, it would not be the first such instance in television history.

I for one refuse to believe that an enterprise so well conceived, so scrupulously produced, and so widely loved can stay boneyarded for long.

And I have 1,898 letters from people who don't believe it either.

JAMES BLISH

Marlow, Bucks, England.
1969

Chapter One

McCOY WITHOUT BONES

From the Captain's Log, Star Date 4011.9:

We are continuing to record a navigation grid for this area of space-time, as directed. Mr. Spock reports that, according to the library, the procedure is still called "bench-marking" after ancient ordinance mapping practices laid down before the days of space flight, though these cubic parsecs of emptiness look like most unattractive sites to park a bench.

Though we are not far by warp drive from the Klingon Empire, and in fact I am sure the Klingons would claim that we were actually in it, the mission has been quite uneventful and I believe I detect some signs of boredom among my officers. Their efficiency, however, seems quite unimpaired.

"What worries me," McCoy said, "is whether I'm myself any more. I have a horrible suspicion that I'm a ghost. And that I've been one for maybe as long as twenty years."

The question caught Captain Kirk's ear as he was crossing the rec room of the *Enterprise* with a handful of coffee. It was not addressed to him, however; turning, he saw that the starship's surgeon was sitting at a table with Scott, who was listening with apparently deep attention. Scotty listening to personal confidences? Or Doc offering them? Ordinarily Scotty had about as

1

much interest in people as his engines might have taken; and McCoy was reticent to the point of cynicism.

"May I join this symposium?" Kirk said. "Or is it private?"

"It's nae private, it's just nonsense, I think," the engineering officer said. "Doc here is developing a notion that the transporter is a sort of electric chair. Thus far, I canna follow him, but I'm trying, I'll do mysel' that credit."

"Oh," Kirk said, for want of anything else to say. He sat down. His first impression, that McCoy had been obliquely referring to his divorce, was now out the porthole, which both restored his faith in his understanding of McCoy's character, and left him totally at sea. Understanding McCoy was a matter of personal as well as ship's importance to Kirk, for as Senior Ship's Surgeon, McCoy was the one man who could himself approach Kirk at any time on the most intimate personal level; indeed, it was McCoy's positive duty to keep abreast of the Captain's physical, mental and emotional condition and to speak out openly about it— and not necessarily only to the patient.

When McCoy joined the *Enterprise*, Kirk suspected that it had been the divorce that had turned him to the Space Service in the first place. The details, however, were a mystery. Kirk did know that McCoy had a daughter, Joanna, who had been twenty back then and for whom the surgeon had provided; she was in training as a nurse somewhere, and McCoy heard from her as often as the interstellar mail permitted. That was not very often.

"Somebody," Kirk said, "had better fill me in. Doc, you've said nine times to the dozen that you don't like the transporter system. In fact, I think 'loath,' is the word you use. 'I do not care to have my molecules scrambled and beamed around as if I were a radio message.' Is this just more of the same?"

"It is and it isn't," McCoy said. "It goes like this. If I understand Scotty aright, the transporter turns our bodies into energy and then reconstitutes them as matter at the destination . . ."

"That's a turrible oversimplification," Scott objected. The presence of his accent, which came out only under stress, was now explained; they were talking about machinery, with which he was actively in love. "What the transporter does is analyze the energy *state* of each particle in the body and then produce a Dirac jump to an equivalent state somewhere else. No conversion is involved—if it were, we'd blow up the ship."

"I don't care about that," McCoy said. "What I care about is my state of consciousness—my ego, if you like. And it isn't matter, energy or anything else I can name, despite the fact that it's the central phenomenon of all human thought. After all, we all know we live in a solipsistic universe."

"A what?" Kirk said.

"We inhabit two universes, then," McCoy said patiently. "One is the universe inside our skulls—our viewpoint universe, as it were. The other is the phenomenal universe—but that in the long run is only a consensus of viewpoint universes, augmented by pointer readings, and other kinds of machine read-outs. The consensus universe is *also* a product of consciousness. Do you agree, Jim?"

"Tentatively," Kirk said. "Except that I find what you call the consensus universe is pretty convincing."

"Statistically, yes. But it breaks down very rapidly when you examine the individual data behind the statistics. All we *really* know is what we register inside our skulls—a theory which used to be called logical positivism. I go further: I say that there may not even be any consensus universe, and that nothing is provably real except my consciousness, which I can't measure. This position is called solipsism, and I say that the fact of self-consciousness forces us all to be solipsists at heart and from birth. We just seldom become aware of it, that's all."

"Space travel does that to you," Kirk agreed. "Especially when you're as far from home as we are now. Luckily, you recover, at least enough to function."

"Nobody ever recovers, completely," McCoy said somberly. "I believe that the first discovery of this situation is one of the great formative shocks in human development—maybe as important as the birth trauma. Tell me, Jim: wasn't there a moment, or an hour, in your childhood or early adolescence when you realized with astonishment that you, the unique and only Jim Kirk, were at the very center of the whole universe? And when you tried to imagine what it would be like to see the universe from some other point of view—that of your father, perhaps—and realized that you were forever a prisoner in your own head?"

Kirk searched his memory. "Yes, there was," he said. "And the fact that I can still remember it, and so easily, does seem to indicate that it was fairly important to me. But after a while I dismissed the whole problem. I couldn't see that it had any practical consequences, and in any event there wasn't anything I could do about it. But you still haven't answered *my* question. What's all this got to do with the transporter?"

"Nary a thing," Scott said.

"On the contrary. Whatever the mechanism, the *effect* of the transporter is to dissolve my body and reassemble it somewhere else. Now you'll agree from experience that this process takes finite, physical time— short, but measurable. Also from experience, that during that time period neither body nor consciousness exists. Okay so far?"

"Well, in a cloudy sort of way," Kirk said.

"Good. Now, at the other end, a body is assembled which is apparently identical with the original, is alive, has consciousness, and has all the memories of the original. *But it is NOT the original.* That has been destroyed."

"I canna see that it matters a whit," Scott said. "Any more than your solipsist position does. As Mr. Spock is fond of saying, 'A difference which *makes* no difference *is* no difference.'"

"No, not to you," McCoy said, "because the new McCoy will look and behave in all respects like the old one. But to me? I can't take so operational a view of the matter. I am, by definition, not the same man who went into a transporter for the first time twenty years ago. I am a construct made by a machine after the image of a dead man—and the hell of it is, not even I can know how exact the imitation is, because—well, because obviously if anything is missing I wouldn't remember it."

"Question," Kirk said. "Do you *feel* any different?"

"Aha," said Scott with satisfaction.

"No, Jim, I don't, but how could I? I *think* I remember what I was like before, but in that I may be vastly mistaken. Psychology is my specialty, for all that you see me chiefly as a man reluctant to hand out pills. I know that there are vast areas of my mind that are inaccessible to my consciousness except under special conditions—under stress, say, or in dreams. What if part of that psychic underground has not been duplicated? How would I know?"

"You could ask Spock," Scott suggested.

"Thanks, no. The one time I was in mind-lock with him it saved my life—it saved all of us, you'll remember—but I didn't find it pleasant."

"Well, you ought to, anyhow," Scott said, "if you're as serious about all this. He could lock onto one of those unconscious areas and then see if it was still there after your next transporter trip."

"Which it almost surely would be," Kirk added. "I don't see why you assume the transporter to be so peculiarly selective. Why should it blot out subconscious traces instead of conscious ones?"

"Why shouldn't it? And in point of fact, does it or doesn't it? That's pretty close to the question I want answered. If it were *the* question, I would even submit to the experiment Scotty proposes, and ask everybody else aboard to as well."

"I," said Kirk, "have been on starship duty somewhat longer than either of you gentlemen. And I will say without qualification that this is the weirdest rec room conversation I've ever gotten into. But all right, Doc, let's bite the bullet. What is *the* question?"

"What would you expect from a psychologist?" McCoy said. "*The* question, of course, is the soul. If it exists, which I know no more than the next man. When I was first reassembled by that damnable machine, did my soul, if any, make the crossing with me—or am I just a reasonable automaton?"

"The ability to worry about the question," Kirk said, "seems to me to be its own answer."

"Hmmm. You may be right, Jim. In fact, you better had be. Because if you aren't, then every time we put a man through the transporter for the first time, we commit murder."

"And thot's nae a haggle, it's a haggis," Scott said hotly. "Look ye, Doc, yon soul's immortal by definition. If it exists, it canna be destroyed—"

"Captain Kirk," said the rec room's intercom speaker.

Kirk arose with some relief; the waters around the table had been getting pretty deep. But his relief was short-lived.

"In the rec room, Mr. Spock."

"Will you relieve me, please, Captain? We are in need of a Command decision."

McCoy and Scott looked up in alarm. A Command decision, out here in a totally unexplored arm of the galaxy?

"I'm on my way," Kirk said. "What, briefly, is the problem?"

"Sir," the first officer's voice said, "the Klingon War has finally broken out. Organia seems already to have been destroyed, and we are cut off from the Federation."

Chapter Two

BEHIND THE LINES

From the Captain's Log, Star Date 4011.8:

This arm of the galaxy has never been visited by human beings, nor by any of the nonhuman races known to us. Our primary mission here was to establish benchmarks for warp-drive flight, and secondarily, of course, to report anything we encountered that might be worth scientific investigation. But now, it would appear, we cannot report at all.

As Kirk entered the bridge, Spock arose from the command chair and moved silently to his own library-computer station. Sulu was at the helm, Lieutenant Uhura at the communications console. The viewing screen showed nothing but stars; the *Enterprise* was in a standard orbit around one of them—Kirk didn't need to care which. All deceptively normal.

"All right, Mr. Spock," Kirk said, sitting down. "The details, please."

"Very sparse, Captain, and more seem impossible to come by," the first officer said. "What little I have is all public knowledge—I have refrained from calling Starfleet Command for obvious reasons. There have been no 'incidents' with the Klingon Empire for over a year, but it now appears that they have mounted a major attack on the Federation along a very broad front—without any prior declaration, naturally. The reports Lieutenant Uhura has received state that Feder-

7

ation forces are holding, but I suggest that we place little confidence in that. Public announcements under such circumstances are always primarily intended to be reassuring, secondarily to mislead the enemy, and may contain only a small residuum of fact."

"Of course," Kirk said. "But such an outbreak was supposed to have been made impossible under the Organian Peace Treaty.* We should know; we were on Organia when the treaty was imposed, and we saw the Organians immobilize both parties in what would otherwise have been a major naval engagement."

"That is true, of course. However, Captain, not only have the Organians failed to intervene this time, but no contact whatsoever can be made with the planet. It seems virtually to have disappeared from the face of the universe. In the absence of any more data, I think we must assume it is destroyed."

Sulu turned partially in his helmsman's chair. "Now how is that possible?" he said. "The Organians were creatures of pure thought. They *couldn't* be destroyed. And it wasn't just one battle they stopped—they simultaneously immobilized fleets all over the galaxy."

"The Organians themselves were thought-creatures," Spock said, "and no doubt much of what we 'saw' on their planet was the result of hypnotism. But we have no real reason to suppose that the planet itself was an illusion; and if it was not, it could be destroyed. What effect that would have on the Organians, we have no idea. All we know is that they have not intervened in the present war, nor does there seem to be any way to find out what has happened to them."

"Well," Kirk said, "let's see what *our* problem is. We've got the whole Klingon Empire between the *Enterprise* and the Federation—including all seventeen Star bases. On the other hand, the Klingons don't know we're here, on their blind side; we might make some capital out of that. Lieutenant Uhura, what are the

---

*See "Errand of Mercy," *Star Trek Two.*

chances of getting some sort of instructions from
Starfleet Command without giving our presence away?"

"Practically nil, Captain," the Bantu girl said. "Even
if we send a query as a microsecond squirt, we'd have
to send it repeatedly and at high gain in order to have
any hope of one such pip being picked up. We've got
the whole of Shapley Center, the heart of the galaxy,
between us and home, and the stellar concentration is
so high there that it makes a considerable energy bulge
even in subspace. To get through all that static, we'd
have to punch out the pips regularly to attract their
attention—and that would attract the Klingons as well.
They wouldn't be able to read the message, but they'd
be able to pinpoint out location all too easily."

"All right," Kirk said. "Send out such a pip *ir*regularly; Mr. Spock, please give Lieutenant Uhura a table
of random numbers from the computer that she can use
as a timetable. Probably it won't work, but we should
try it. In the meantime, we have to assume that whatever we do is entirely up to us—and that if we're to be of
any help at all to the Federation, we'll have to do it
fast. I assume to begin with that we can rule out trying
to circumnavigate the whole Klingon Empire."

"I would certainly agree," Spock said. "By the time
we completed such a trip, or even got within safe
hailing distance of the Federation or any Starbase, the
war would probably be over."

"We could try to smash our way directly through,"
Sulu said. "We do have a lot of fire-power, plus the
advantage of surprise. And on this side, the Empire is
hardly fortified at all—think what a mess we could
make of their supply bases, their communications, their
whole rear echelon. It would be all out of proportion to
the amount of damage a starship could do in a conventional battle situation, against matched enemy forces."

"It would also," Kirk said grimly, "get us ambushed,
eventually."

"Maybe not for a long while," Sulu said. "We could
do it hit-and-run. I could plot us a course—maybe

using a random-number table again—I'd defy any computer to predict."

"You couldn't do that and hit important targets at the same time," Kirk said, "or work closer to the Federation; and if the course isn't truly random, it can be predicted. And the closer we got to the Federation the closer we'd get to the battle front *on the wrong side*. We'd be blown out of space before we could cross."

"The damage we might do," Spock said, "might well be worth the price to the Federation. Mr. Sulu's suggestion has considerable merit from a strategic point of view."

"And I'm willing to entertain the idea if I have to," Kirk said. "But it's clearly a suicidal tactic. My responsibility is to the ship and the crew, as well as to the Federation. I'm not about to lose the *Enterprise* and everybody aboard her on such a venture, without direct orders from the Federation to do so. If I receive such orders, I'll obey them; without such orders, I veto the scheme. Has anybody another notion?"

"There exists what I would call an intermediate possibility, Captain," Spock said. "It depends from a rather shaky chain of logic, but it may be the best we can manage."

"Let's hear it."

"Very well. We can safely assume, first of all, that the Klingons would not have risked starting the war without feeling some assurance that they had the Federation outmatched both in fire-power and fire-control. No one but a berserker would start a war under any other circumstances, and the Klingons, while warlike in the extreme, are not berserkers.

"Subpoint one: We may assume that the Klingons have new weapons, as well as what they believe to be a preponderance of familiar ones. But we do not know what these might be.

"Main point two: Since the Organians have forbidden any such war and had the power to stop it, it follows that the Klingons would not have started it unless they had advance knowledge that the Organians were out of commission.

"Subpoint two: This knowledge may be in itself the most important of the new weapons in the Klingons' hands. However . . .

"Conclusion: At least a forty per cent probability that the Klingons have used a new weapon which *caused* the immobilization or destruction of Organia."

"Whew," Sulu said. "I was following you, Mr. Spock, but I sure didn't suspect that that was where you were going."

"Where do you get your probability figure?" Uhura asked. "I didn't hear any such parameters in your premises."

"One may diagram an argument of this type as a series of overlapping circles," Spock said. "When you eliminate those parts of the circles which lie outside the area they have in common . . ."

"Never mind that," Kirk said. "What you've given us thus far is only the logical chain you mentioned. Do you have a course of action to recommend?"

"Certainly."

"All right. Uhura, call Dr. McCoy and Mr. Scott up here. I don't want to go any farther until they've been filled in."

This was not very time-consuming, since Spock had recorded the whole conversation, as he routinely did any discussion preliminary to a Command decision. Scott and the surgeon listened to the recording intently.

"All clear, Doc? Scotty? Any questions? All right, Mr. Spock; what is your proposed course of action?"

The first officer said, "Why not go to Organia, instead of to any Starbase, and try to find out what exactly *has* happened there? Such a course has almost all of the tactical advantages invoked by Mr. Sulu—it would vastly disorganize the Klingons' rear echelon, through sheer surprise and the military weakness of this side of the Empire. Furthermore, we would be going in an unexpected direction; once the Klingons detected us, they would naturally expect us to be bent upon rejoining the Fleet, or getting under the protection of the heavy guns of a Starbase. That Organia was our actual destination would probably be their third guess, and it might well be their fifth or sixth. Finally, the possible *strategic* advantage can hardly be overestimated: should we succeed in finding out what happened to Organia, *and doing something about it,* the war would be ended."

"Unless," McCoy added, "what happened to Organia turns out to be irreparable except by God."

"I offer no guarantees," Spock said evenly. "Only possibilities."

"I rather like the proposal," Kirk said slowly. "The risk is still enormous, of course, but at least the scheme isn't outright suicidal. Mr. Spock, I need two computations: first, transit time to Organia from our present coordinates at Warp Six; and second, transit time to territorial space of the Empire on the same line of flight."

Spock turned to his hooded station, and said after a moment, "We would officially enter Klingon space in two months, and the remaining transit time to Organia would be four months more. Of course, there is always the chance that the Klingons may be patrolling beyond their own territory, but I estimate the probability as low on this side of the Empire."

It could be worse, Kirk realized. Here was one Command decision which was actually going to allow him the luxury of reflection; only a partial decision was required right now, on the spot. He had, apparently, a minimum of a whole month in which to change his mind.

But all he said was, "Mr. Sulu, lay course for Organia at Warp Six. Lieutenant Uhura, extend all sensors to maximum range, beginning now, and tie in an automatic full battle alert to anything that might indicate another ship. Also, call me at once should anything come through from Starfleet Command."

"Of course, Captain," the communications officer said.

But in fact nothing did come through, which was scarcely surprising. Though it was normal for a starship to be out of touch with the Federation hierarchy for long periods, the sheer volume of messages which came in daily to Starfleet Command was nevertheless vast, and the chances of picking up an unscheduled message in a microsecond pip—a message, furthermore, which did not dare to call attention to itself—correspondingly tiny. As was also usual, Kirk was going to have to play this one on his own judgment alone.

He observed, however, that there was some unusual activity going on in the ship's computation section. Scotty evidently had a problem of considerable complexity; for nearly a week he was in earnest conference with Spock, armed with sheafs of, to begin with, equations, and later, rough engineering specs. Kirk left them to themselves. Whatever they were doing, they were not wasting their time, that was certain; and he would hear about it in good order.

And at the end of the week, Scott in fact requested an interview with Kirk in the Captain's working quarters.

"Captain, d'ye recall our chatter with Doc about the transporter, an' his various misgivin's?"

"Yes, Scotty, though I can't say it has been losing me any sleep."

"Weel, ah dinna been fashin' mysel' over the moral part of it, either. But I got to thinkin' it was a vurra pretty technical problem, an' what I've come up with the noo seems to have a bearin' on our present situation."

"Somehow I'm not surprised," Kirk said. "Tell me about it."

"D'ye ken what tachyons are?"

"I was told about them in school. As I recall, they're particles that travel faster than light—for which nobody's ever found any use."

"An' that's the truth, but only part of it. Tachyons *canna* travel any *slower* than light, and what their top speed might be has nae been determined. They exist in what's called Hilbert space, which has as many dimensions as ye need to assume for the solvin' of any particular problem. An' for every particle in normal space—be it proton, electron, positron, neutron, nae matter what—there's an equivalent tachyon."

"That," Kirk said, "is already a lot more than my instructor seemed to know about them."

"A lot has been discovered since then. I had to have a refresher course from Mr. Spock mysel', believe me. But it's aye important. Suppose we were to redesign the transporter so that, instead of scannin' a man an' replicatin' him at destination in his normal state, it replicated him in tachyons, at *this* end of the process? That would solve the moral problem, because the original subject wouldna go anywhere—while the tachyon creature, which canna exist in the everyday universe with us, would go on to destination and revert to normal there. No murder, if such be in fact the problem, ever occurs."

"Hmm. It seems to me . . ."

"Wait, Captain, there's more. The method vastly extends the range of the transporter. I canna tell you exactly how far, but our present sixteen-thousand-mile limit would be the flight of a gnat by comparison.

"Result? We send a man to Organia *from here*. He gathers the data we need; when he returns to the ship, we hold him in the tachyon state for as long as is needed to yield up the material. Then we let the field go, and *poof!* The replica becomes so much tachyon plasma in another universe, and our original has never even left the ship!"

"Obviously," Kirk said slowly, "you wouldn't be bringing this to me if you weren't sure you had the mechanics solved."

"That's the fact, Captain, and it's aye proud of oursel' we are, too," Scott said. "Geniuses we are, an' you may gi'e us medals at your convenience. But seriously, it will work, an' we can do it. To modify the machine itself is the work of a week—an' we needn't travel another inch closer to the Klingon Empire than we are by then."

"We'll go on traveling anyhow," Kirk said. "I like to have choices open."

"To be sure—my hyperbole was showin'."

Kirk clicked on the intercom. "Kirk here. Mr. Spock, place the ship on full automatic control. All department heads to the briefing room at zero point seven this day. Kirk out." The intercom went off. "Mr. Scott, proceed with your alterations of the transporter—making sure in the process that they're not permanent."

"Vurra good," Scott said, getting up. Kirk raised his hand.

"But," he added, "if I were you, I wouldn't tell Dr. McCoy that I'd solved his moral problem."

"No?"

"No. You see, Scotty, he's likely to ask you if the tachyon replicate has an immortal soul—and somehow I don't think you'd be in a position to answer."

Chapter Three

THE TANK TRAP

From the Captain's Log, Star Date 4018.4:

Upon assurance from Mr. Scott that there was no bodily danger inherent in his transporter modification, Mr. Spock was chosen as the logical emissary to Organia. He was on the planet during the entire affair which led to the treaty (see Log entry Star Date 3199.4), and personally knows Ayelborne, Claymare and Trefayne—or at least knows the humanoid shapes they assume, as his is known to them. The only other person thus qualified is myself. In addition, Mr. Spock is probably the closest observer of us all.

There was a number of transporter rooms in various parts of the *Enterprise*, but it was the main one that Scott modified, for the obvious reason: power. Of all the modifications, only one was immediately visible, although Kirk was in no doubt that there were other changes on the free-standing console of which the Transporter Officer and his technician were aware. The circular platform of the transporter chamber itself had been enclosed in gleaming metal, so that its six positions could no longer be seen—only the steps leading up to them.

"The shielding unfortunately is necessary," the engineering officer explained to Kirk and Spock. "As long as the field is on, the whole interior of the chamber is effectively in another universe—or more exactly, in a kind of continuum in which a transfinite number and variety of universes are possible—and the effect has to be confined. I could just as well have used wire mesh—for instance, shuttlecraft landing-pad web—so we could see in, but I had the armor plate to hand from another job and I was in a hurry, as I assume we all are."

Scott's burr vanished completely when he was trying to be as precise as possible. Kirk was thoroughly used to this, but nevertheless it seldom failed to make him smile.

"That'll do for now, Scotty. We can add frills later. In fact, if this works as you've predicted, engineers all over the galaxy will be thinking up refinements for it. For now, what exactly is the program?"

"Pretty much as it always is, Captain, except for the distance involved. We set up the coordinates on the console—by the way, Mr. Spock, what are they?"

"Eleven eight seventy d. y. by eighty-five seventy-four sixty-eight K."

The Transporter Officer looked astonished—evidently Scott had not yet filled him in on "the distance involved"—but made no comment. Scott went on.

"Then Mr. Spock steps into the tank, and stands on any station; we close the door and activate the machine. He won't notice a thing, for though he'll be momentarily surrounded by n-dimensional space, he's only equipped to perceive four at a time, like the rest of us. But he won't disappear—he'll just step out of the tank again. In the meantime, his replicate will be on its way to Organia, and will be returned here automatically, one day after materialization, no matter when that takes place. If that's not a long enough stay, we'll send him back. When the replicate arrives here, we'll again have established Hilbert space in the tank, and will maintain it for as long as it takes the replica to report."

"Clear enough for now," Kirk said. "Mr. Spock, are you ready?"

"Yes, Captain."

"Into the tank with you then," Scott said.

Spock entered, and the door closed behind him. The

transporter officer manipulated the controls. As Scott had predicted, there was nothing to be seen, nor did the familiar muted whine of the transporter field seem changed in any way. Kirk tried to imagine what an n-dimensional space would be like, and was not surprised to fail.

"That's all there is to it," Scott said. "He can come out now."

Spock, however, failed to appear. Kirk said, "We seem to have forgotten to arrange any way to let him know that. I assume it's safe to open the door now?"

"Entirely, Captain."

Kirk went to the platform and slid the door back. "Mr. Spock . . ."

Then he stopped. Spock was there, all right, and apparently quite unharmed. In fact, he was one hundred per cent too much there.

There were two identical Spocks in the tank.

The two Spocks were eyeing each other with a mixture of wariness and disdain, like a man trying to fathom the operation of a trick mirror. Kirk was sure that his own expression was a good deal less judicious.

"Which of you," he demanded, "is the original?"

"I am, Captain," both Spocks said, in chorus.

"I was afraid you'd say that. Well, let's get one problem settled right now. Hereafter, I will address *you*," he pointed to the man on his left, "as Spock One, and *you*," he pointed to his right, "as Spock Two. This implies no decision on my part as to which of you is in fact the original. Scotty, obviously you didn't anticipate any such outcome."

"Nay, I dinna," Scott said. " 'Tis a pity we couldna see into the tank now, since otherwise we'd know which was which by the station he's on."

"Can you determine that?" Kirk asked the transporter officer.

"No, sorry, sir, I can't. Under this new setup, all the stations were activated at once."

"And Scotty, equally obviously *neither* of them can be tachyon constructs."

"Thot's aye eempossible," Scott agreed unhappily.

"Then the next task is to figure out how and why this happened, and if possible, discover some way to distinguish between the original and the replicate. With *two* Spocks on this ship, I must say, there ought to be no logical problem we can't lick."

"Unless," Spock One said, "we think exactly alike, in which case the replicate is simply a superfluity."

"Quite obviously you don't think exactly alike," Kirk said, "or both of you would have offered that remark simultaneously and in the same words."

"True but not relevant, Captain, if I may so observe," said Spock Two. "Even if we thought exactly alike at the moment of creation of the replicate, from then on our experiences differ slightly—beginning, of course, with the simple difference that we occupy different positions in space-time. This will create a divergence in our thinking which will inevitably widen as time goes on."

"The difference, however, may remain trivial for some significant time to come," said Spock One.

"We are already disagreeing, are we not?" Spock Two said coldly. "That is already a nontrivial difference."

"That's enough cross talk, both of you," Kirk said. "You certainly both sound like the real Spock, as well as look like him, and as far as I'm concerned, you're creating twice the confusion he did on his worst logic jags. Spock One, go to your quarters and remain there until I call you. Spock Two, come with me to *my* quarters."

Neither man spoke further until turboelevator and corridors brought them to Kirk's workroom, where Kirk waved the problematical second First Officer to the chair before his desk.

"Now then," the Captain said. "first of all, did you in fact get to Organia for even a fraction of a second? And if so, did you see anything useful?"

"No, Captain. Nothing happened except that suddenly there were two Spocks in the chamber. And I can tell you positively that there is no hiatus in my memory at that point."

"I'm sorry to hear it—not only because we need the information badly, but because it might have provided a clue for telling the two of you apart. You still maintain that you are the original Spock, I suppose?"

"I do," Spock Two said, in the tone he generally reserved for reporting an established fact of nature.

"Well, you see what the situation is as well as I do. While I suppose I could learn to live with two Mr. Spocks aboard—I might even come to like it—the ship cannot tolerate two first officers. Which of you do I demote, and to what post, and on what grounds?"

Spock Two raised his eyebrows. "May I suggest, Captain, that the situation is far more serious than that? To take a relatively minor aspect of it first, perhaps you can learn to live with two Spocks, but it would be somewhat painful for me. If you will imagine what it would be like for you to have a second James T. Kirk abroad in the universe, you will readily understand why."

"Hmm. Yes—personally it would be highly unpleasant. Your pardon, Mr. Spock. I just hadn't had enough time to ponder that aspect of it."

"I quite understand. But there is a second derivative. It would be positively dangerous to the ship. I am not speaking now of the confusion which it would produce, though that would be bad enough in itself, but of the effect upon the efficiency of the first officer. While I shall learn to endure the situation if you so order—even should I wind up as a yeoman—whichever of us remains first officer would be operating under continual personal stress about which he could do nothing at all. Suppose, for instance, it occurs to him that the demoted Spock is conspiring to replace him? Or consider, Captain, the position in which you would find yourself, should the demoted Spock suddenly charge that he is the one you retained as first officer, and that the other man has slipped into his place unobserved? Such an exchange, or a series of them, might well evolve simply from a sense of duty on the part of each man."

Kirk whistled. "Now *that* would demoralize everybody, including me, even under peacetime conditions. You're right, I don't see how we dare risk it. But what would you suggest we do instead?"

"You have no choice, Captain. You must destroy one of us."

Kirk stared at him for a long minute. At last he said, "Even if it turns out to be you?"

"Even," Spock Two said levelly, "if it is I."

There was an even longer silence, while Kirk thought about the emotional consequences to himself of such a course. It did not make pleasant thinking. But what were the alternatives? The case Spock Two had offered seemed airtight.

"I may in fact do that," Kirk said finally. "But only if we can work out some foolproof way of determining which of you is the original. In the meantime, please, go directly to the bridge, remain there for ten minutes precisely, and then retire to your quarters until further notice."

His expression shuttered, Spock Two nodded once and left. The moment the door closed behind him, Kirk opened the intercom and called Spock's quarters. "Kirk calling Mr. Spock One."

"Here, Captain."

"Please report directly to my quarters at once."

When Spock One entered, Kirk realized with a shock just how grave the identity problem actually was. Had Spock Two, after closing the door, simply walked down the corridor until he was out of sight from Kirk's quarters, then turned around and come back at a leisurely pace and announced himself as Spock One, there would have been no immediate way for Kirk to have known that it had happened. And, now that Kirk came to think of it . . .

"Sit down, Mr. Spock. Kirk to the bridge!"

"Uhura here, Captain."

"Is Mr. Spock there?"

Spock One raised his eyebrows, but said nothing.

"No, Captain, it's not his watch. As a matter of fact he did drop in for about five minutes, but he just left. You might try his quarters—or shall I page him for you?"

"No thanks, Lieutenant, nothing urgent. Kirk out."

One minor crisis averted—or had it been? He had told Spock Two to stay on the bridge for ten minutes, but Uhura said he had left after five. No, that probably meant nothing; people who are busy seldom notice how long spectators are around, and almost never know, or care, how long ago they left. Scratch that—but there would be hundreds of other such cruxes. Uhura, for instance, like almost all the rest of the crew, did not even know yet what had happened in the Transporter room.

"Mr. Spock, beginning now, I want you to wear some identifying mark, and see to it that it's unique and never leaves your person."

"Then you had better invent it, Captain. Anything that I might choose might also occur to the replicate. And perhaps it should also be unobtrusive, at least for the time being."

That made sense; Spock One did not want to confuse the more than four hundred and thirty members of the crew with two First Officers until such confusion could no longer be avoided. Neither did Kirk, though he was painfully aware that concealing the problem might equally well compound it.

Kirk drew off his class ring and passed it over. "Use that—and give me your own Command Academy ring. Your, uh, counterpart also has one, of course, but it won't pass for mine on close inspection. There are no others on this vessel, that I'm sure."

"No, Captain, no other officer on the *Enterprise* ever even stood for Command, as the computer will verify."

"I'll check it. And again, you're not to regard this exchange as a sign of preference from me—that issue is far from settled. The exchange is for my convenience only."

"I quite understand, Captain. A logical precaution."

Kirk winced. They *both* were Spock, right down to characteristic turns of phrase and nuances of attitude.

"Good. Now let's get down to the hard rock. I've been talking to Spock Two, and we've made a certain amount of progress—though not in a direction I like very much. It wouldn't surprise me if you'd come to very much the same conclusions he did—but on the other hand, the two of you were disagreeing earlier on, so I'd prefer to rehearse what we said. Briefly, it went like this . . ."

Spock One listened to the Captain's account with complete expressionlessness and immobility; but when he was asked for his opinion, Kirk got the next of his many shocks of the day.

"May I suggest, Captain," Spock One said, "that it is illogical to expect me to view this line of argument with c-complete equanimity? To begin with, you and I are friends—a fact I have never intentionally exploited in any duty situation, but a fact of long standing nevertheless. To find that you would agree to kill any Spock cannot but distort my judgment."

Kirk, too, listened immobile and without expression, but had he been a cat, his ears would have swiveled straight forward on his head. The hesitations in Spock One's speech were extremely faint indeed, but, for Spock, they were utterly unprecedented; to Kirk the effect was as startling as though his first officer had been positively stuttering with indignation.

Kirk said carefully, "You were ready to kill *me* on one occasion.* In fact, for a while, you thought you had."

It was a fearfully cruel thing to have to say; but the time for politeness seemed to be well past.

"I recall that with no pride, Jim, I assure you,"

*See "Amok Time" *Star Trek Three.*

Spock One said, with a kind of stony ruefulness nobody but a man half Vulcan and half human could even have felt, let alone expressed. "But you in turn will recall that I was amok at the time, because of the mating ceremony. Do you wish me back in that irrational state of mind? Or want me to welcome something similar in you?"

"Of course not. Quite the opposite. What I want from you now is the best logic you've ever been able to bring to bear, on any situation whatsodamnever."

"Nothing else will serve, Captain, it seems to me. So let me further observe that my counterpart's proposal is not conservative. There is a certain justice in his observation that our joint presence on the ship will be disturbing for both of us, but we are not likely to be disturbed about the same subjects at the same time; hence you could use both of us by asking both our opinions, and striking a balance between them." The ghostly hesitation was gone now—had Kirk imagined it in the first place? "Furthermore, Captain, this whole question of identity is operationally meaningless. I can assure you that I *know* I am the original—but this knowledge is not false even if I am in fact the replicate."

"You'll have to explain further, I'm afraid." But the difficulty of the argument was in itself reassuringly Spocklike—falsely reassuring, Kirk knew with regret.

"If I am the replicate, I have a complete, continuous set of memories which were replicated with me. As far as I can know, all these memories represent real experiences, and there is no break in continuity in them, nor in my attitudes or abilities. Therefore, both for my purposes *and for yours,* either of us is the original, and there is no reason to prefer one over the other. A difference which makes no difference is no difference."

"McCoy's Paradox," Kirk said.

"Is that one of the classic paradoxes? I am not familiar with it. I was quoting Korzybski."

"No, Doc invented it only two weeks ago—but abruptly it has come to life." Kirk paused. He was not himself expert in logic, and now he was confronted by two experts, each arguing opposite sides of a life-and-death problem, and with apparently equal cogency. "Mr. Spock, I shall of course inform you when I've made my decision, but it's not a matter on which I want to shoot from the hip. For the present, I want you and your counterpart to stand alternate half-day watches. That way, I get both your services continuously, I don't have to choose between you yet, and I don't have to flip a coin to decide which of you has to be moved out of your quarters."

"An ideal interim solution," Spock One said, arising.

For you, maybe, Kirk thought as he watched him go out. *But your—brother—wants you dead.*

He sighed and touched the intercom. "Doc? Kirk here. Break out the headache pills, I'm coming to pay you a visit."

Chapter Four

A PROBLEM IN DETECTION

From the Captain's Log, Star Date 4019.2:

I have appraised the Department heads of the situation and asked for suggestions. For the time being I have not informed the rest of the crew, in the interests of morale. Since any given one of them is seldom on the bridge, I am spared having to explain away the odd spectacle of Mr. Spock on duty all ten periods of the day.

To this decision, however, Kirk had to allow two exceptions. One was Yeoman Janice Rand, who served Kirk as a combination of executive secretary, valet and military aide, and as such was usually made privy to anything that was going on; ordinarily she needed to know, and in any event it was a lot easier to tell her how matters stood than to keep them from her. The other was Christine Chapel, McCoy's head nurse; not only was she Doc's surgical assistant, but she held several degrees in medical research, and hence would be closely involved in whatever attempts McCoy might invent to distinguish one Spock from another.

Both were highly professional career woman, co-equal with male crewmen of the same rank during duty hours and expected to deliver the same level of efficient performance. Neither, however, was able to suppress a certain gleam of anticipation on being told that there were now two Spocks aboard the Starship USS *Enterprise*.

With Yeoman Rand, this was only normal and natural. She practiced a protective, freewheeling interest in men in general to keep herself and the Captain from becoming dangerously involved with each other. Kirk was, however, surprised to see it in Nurse Chapel. She came as close to being a professional confidant as the irascible McCoy was ever likely to find; acting both as a bond between them and a preventive against its transgressing onto the personal was the fact that she, too, was the veteran of a broken romance, and from it had apparently found a measure of contentment in a Starfleet Service.

What was the source of the oddly overt response that women of all ages and degrees of experience seemed to feel toward Spock? Kirk had no answer, but he had two theories, switching from one to the other according to his mood. One was that it was a simple challenge-and-response situation: he may be cold and unresponsive to other women, but if *I* had the chance, *I* could get through to him! The other, more complex theory seemed more plausible to Kirk only in his moments of depression: that most white crewwomen, still the inheritors after two centuries of vestiges of the shameful racial prejudices of their largely Anglo-American forebears, saw in the Vulcan half-breed—who after all had not sprung from any *Earthly* colored stock—a "safe" way of breaking with those vestigial prejudices—and at the same time, perhaps, satisfying the sexual curiosity which had probably been at the bottom of them from the beginning.

McCoy, once Kirk had broached both these notions to him—on shore leave, after several drinks—had said, "You parlor psychologists are all alike—constantly seeking for complexities and dark, hidden motives where none probably exist. Most people are simpler than that, Jim. Our Mr. Spock, much though I hate to admit it, is a thoroughly superior specimen of the male animal—brave, intelligent, prudent, loyal, highly placed in his society—you name it, he's got it. What sensible woman *wouldn't* want such a man? But women are also practical creatures, and skeptical about men. They can see that Spock's not a whole man. That compulsive inability of his to show his emotions cripples him, and they want to try to free him of it. Little do they know what a fearful task it would be."

"Oh. So in part it's the mother instinct, too?"

McCoy made an impatient face. "There you go again, applying tags you don't understand. I wish you'd leave the psychology to me—what's the Service paying me for, anyhow, if you can do it? Oh well, never mind. Jim, if you're really puzzled about this, watch the women for once! You'll see for yourself that mothering Spock is the *last* thing they have in mind. No—they want to free him to be the whole, grownup, near-superman he hasn't quite become, and make themselves good enough for that man. And as I said before, they don't know how much they'd have to bite off before they could chew it."

"The Vulcan cultural background?" Kirk said.

"Yes, for a starter. But there's a lot more. Did you know, Jim, that if Spock weren't half Vulcan, I'd be watching him now every day for signs of cancer?"

"I thought that had been licked a hundred years ago."

"No, some kinds still show up. And men of one hundred per cent Earth stock, who have avenues for emotional discharge as inadequate as Mr. Spock's are terribly susceptible to it in their middle years. Nobody knows why."

The conversation continued to branch off, leaving Kirk, as usual, with most of his questions unanswered. Nor had McCoy been half as positive about his chances for setting up suitable physiological tests to distinguish between the duplicate Spocks.

"I don't know how the replication happened, so I don't know where to begin. And I was never trained in the details of Vulcanian biochemistry. I read up on it after Spock first came aboard, but most of what I know about it from experience I learned from monitoring him; and he's a mixture, a hybrid, and hence a law unto himself. Oh, of course I'll try to think of something, but dammitall, this is really a problem in physics —I need Scotty for the whats, hows and whys of the accident to get even a start on it!"

"I was afraid of that," Kirk said.

"There's something else you ought to watch out for, though."

"What's that?"

"It's a psychological problem—this business of being identical twins. Even under ordinary, biological circumstances, being an identical twin is a hard row to hoe. You're constantly having identity trouble; mothers think it's cute to dress the kids alike, teachers have trouble keeping their records straight, friends can't tell them apart or think it's funny to pretend they can't. It all usually comes to a head in puberty, which is when the who-am-I problem becomes acute for everyone, but for identical twins it's hell. If they get through that period without becoming neurotic or worse, they're usually all right from then on.

"But Spock didn't go through it, and furthermore, he has been emotionally isolated almost all his life, by his own choice. Now, suddenly, he has been twinned as an adult, and it's a situation he has had no chance to adjust to, as the natural twin has. The strain is going to be considerable."

Kirk spread his hands. "Help him if he'll let you, of course, Doc, and I'll try to take it into account myself. But it seems to me that the adjustment is almost wholly something he'll have to arrive at by himself. And bear in mind that he *has* had a lifetime of training in controlling his own emotions."

"Not controlling them—suppressing them," McCoy said. "The two are very different. But of course he'll have to handle it by himself. One thing laymen never understand about psychotherapy is that no doctor has ever cured an emotional or mental upset, or ever will; the best he can do is to show the patient how he might cure himself.

"But Jim, don't minimize this—it's no small consid-

eration. In my judgment, there's likely to be a real
emotional crisis, and sooner rather than later. I've already noticed that one of them's gone considerably off
his feed. Won't hurt him for a while—Vulcans can fast
a long time—but anorexia is almost always the first sign
of an emotional upset."

"Thanks," Kirk said grimly. "I'll be on my guard.
And in the meantime, let's see if Scotty's thought of any
tests yet."

He left the sick bay and went to the engineering
bridge.

"Scotty, I hate to keep taxing you with the same old
question, but Doc says he can't get anywhere on setting
up a test for the real Spock, or the replicate, until he
has at least some sort of idea of how the duplication
happened. Any clues yet?"

Scott said miserably, "Ah dinna ken, Captain. Ah
dinna oonderstahnd it at all."

There were blue-black isometric smudges under his
eyes, and it was obvious that he had not slept at all
since the start of the botched transporter experiment.
Kirk stopped pressing him at once; clearly he was doing
his best, and his performance wouldn't be improved by
distracting him.

Then everybody, not just Scott, was interrupted by
the call to Battle Stations.

Kirk's immediate assumption—that Uhura's sensors
had picked up something that might be another ship—
proved to be true, but he was no sooner on the bridge
than he became aware that this was only a small part of
the story. For one thing, the automatic drive log on his
control console showed that the *Enterprise* had been off
warp flight for a split second before the alarm had
sounded. She was now back in subspace, of course, but
the trace the sensors had picked up was that of an
object so small that if it had really been a Klingon ship
it would have been incapable of detecting the *Enterprise* in subspace over the distance involved.

"What," Kirk demanded grimly, "were we doing off warp drive?"

"The computer took us off," Sulu said, with the justifiable irritation of the helmsman who has had control snatched away from him by a brainless mechanism. "It still seems to be operating on the old bench-marking schedule. Maybe in all the subsequent confusion, nobody ever told it we were going to Organia."

"That's flatly impossible," Kirk said. "I logged that order myself. Somebody had to countermand it. Mr. Spock, ask the machine who did."

The First Officer—it was Spock Two who was on duty—turned to the console, and then said, "The computer reports that I gave the order, Captain, as is only logical. But in point of fact I deny doing so—and I strongly suspect that my counterpart will also deny it."

"Wipe that order, and see that it stays wiped. Mr. Sulu, put us back on warp drive on the double."

"Already on, Captain."

"Mr. Spock, is the computer malfunctioning?"

"No, Captain, it is in perfect order. There is no doubt that one of us did so instruct it. But since such a course clearly involves grave risks of detection by the Klingons, and has no compensatory advantages, it can only have been given because detection was exactly what was hoped for. That is why I conclude that my counterpart will also deny having given it."

"The argument applies with equal force to you," Kirk pointed out.

"I am thoroughly aware of that. Unfortunately, however, there is no other reasonable explanation."

"No time is recorded for the issuance of the order, I suppose."

"No, which further argues that the issuer wished to remain unknown."

Kirk thought a moment. "Lieutenant Uhura, any sign that we have in fact been detected?"

"I think so, Captain. If the object has laid any sensors on us, they're too feeble to register on my board—but it dropped into subspace just after we did, so it can't be a natural object and may well be following us—though at a *very* respectful distance."

"Mr. Sulu, execute some simple, showy evasive maneuvers and see if it follows those. If it does, lose it—or if you can't lose it, outrun it. It can't pack enough power to pace us."

"I'll lose it," Sulu promised cheerfully.

"Mr. Spock, you are relieved of all duties. Mr. Sulu is designated first officer *pro tem*. Lieutenant Uhura, notify all concerned that henceforth and until further notice, orders from either Spock are without authority aboard this ship. We are proceeding to Organia as before, and until I say otherwise; the bench-marking program is cancelled. Any questions?"

There were none.

"Mr. Spock, call your counterpart in your quarters and notify him that we're *both* coming to visit him. In the interest of ship's harmony I've been trying to avoid such confrontations, but one of you has driven me to the wall—me, and himself."

Kirk had not been in the first officer's quarters since the incident of Spock's near-marriage on Vulcan itself—the painful episode Kirk had obliquely referred to in his first interview with Spock One, the episode during which an amok Spock had quite seriously tried to kill him. These quarters were very like his own in general plan, but considerably more austere. What little decoration they sported consisted chiefly of a few pieces of cutlery, vaguely and misleadingly Oriental in design, which reminded Kirk that Spock's parental culture—on his father's side though now fiercely rationalistic in its biases—had once been almost equally fiercely military.

Kirk was not surprised to notice that the quarters showed not the slightest sign that they were being occupied by two people instead of one. There were two Spocks here now, however, and they were staring at each other with cold but undisguised hostility. The battle had been joined, overtly, at last. Perhaps that was just as well.

"One of you two gentlemen has been uncharacteristically stupid," Kirk said, "and if I could detect which one it was, I'd fire him out the emergency airlock in his underwear. Wantonly endangering the *Enterprise* is as serious a crime as violating General Order Number One, as far as I'm concerned—and as you both know very well. So I'm at open war with one of you, and both of you are going to have to suffer for it. Spock One, did you countermand a course order that I'd logged in the computer?"

"No, Captain, certainly not."

"A routine question. Very well. You are relieved of duty, both of you, and I wish you joy in trying to stay out of each other's hair in the same quarters with nothing to do. In the meantime, I've got no grounds to want to cause either of you selective discomfort, if you know what I mean, and I'll try to see that I don't. In return, I want your advice. Spock One, do you agree that whoever had the computer take us off warp drive wanted the *Enterprise* detected by the Klingons?"

"It seems to be the only possible conclusion," Spock One said.

"Why did he do it?"

"I can only guess, Captain. It is conceivable that the original Spock did after all reach Organia and found it occupied by the Klingons—or was intercepted by the Klingons in some other way—and that a double who was actually a Klingon agent was sent back along with the original. The fact that no memory of this exists in the original's mind, nor any evidence of mental tampering, is not diagnostic; we are dealing with totally new and unknown forces here, as Mr. Scott's bafflement makes very evident.'"

"The possibility certainly can't be discounted," Kirk agreed. "And it does offer a motive for what happened with the computer. Spock Two, any comments?"

"One word, if I may, Captain," Spoct Two said. "The word is: *nonsense.*"

"Again, why?"

"Because it involves too many *ad hoc* assumptions.

William of Occam, one of Earth's pioneers in scientific method, established that one must not multiply logical entities without sufficient reason. The principle is now called the Law of Parsimony."

"Currently rephrased to read, the simplest explanation that fits all the facts is the preferable one," Kirk said. "Have you got a simpler?"

"I think so," said Spock Two. "There is no evidence that the original Spock was ever transported anywhere. It is far simpler to suppose that what we see is in fact the case: that something went wrong with the new process and materialized a mirror image. If this is what happened, it would involve the deepest levels of the replicate's nervous system, producing a reversal of personality as well—and there would be the source of your motive for sympathy with the Klingons."

"Spock One, what do you say to that notion?"

"It has the virtue of simplicity," Spock One said coldly, "and as such is clearly to be preferred. But Occam's Razor is only a human preference, not a natural law. And this mirror hypothesis is also an assumption for which no hard evidence exists."

"Granted," said Spock Two. "But may I point out, Captain, that though each of these assumptions excludes the other, both nevertheless argue toward the same course of action: the *immediate* destruction of the replicate."

"Provided both assumptions are not equally wrong," Spock One said.

"Or providing one of them is right," Kirk said, "Either leaves me with the same question I had before: *Which is the replicate?*"

Neither Spock answered him—and he would not have believed them if they had.

Chapter Five

ON THE OTHER HAND . . .

From the Captain's Log, Star Date 4020.8:

I have interdicted further orders from either Spock until the identity question can be resolved—if it can be— although it effectively deprives me of my first officer. This is a long way from being even a satisfactory interim move, however, since even without authority an alienated Spock could work all kinds of mischief. But there is no way of preventing this short of throwing both of them in the brig, a step for which I have no present grounds.

Operating without a first officer was exhausting work despite Sulu's best efforts, especially under the added strain of Klingon surveillance—Sulu had indeed managed to shake the scout ship that had been trailing the *Enterprise,* but there could be no doubt that the Klingons now knew she was somewhere in the area, and would be searching for her grimly, tenaciously and efficiently. Nevertheless, when Kirk came off watch he went to the sick bay before turning in.

"Something that Spock Two suggested has been nagging at me," he told McCoy. "If the replicate is in fact a mirror image, wouldn't fluoroscopy or an X-ray show it? Heart pointing the wrong way, appendix on the left side, something like that?"

"Afraid not, Jim," McCoy said. "Anatomically, Vulcans have perfect bilateral symmetry—and no appendix, either. Of course, Spock is genetically half human, but the only influence that has in this particular area is in handedness."

"I thought of that, but obviously the replicate has thought of it too. If he's in fact left-handed, he's counterfeiting being right-handed very successfully."

"Let's keep watching for it anyhow. Handedness is a very deep physiological bias—sooner or later he's bound to slip."

"Spock? You must be kidding."

"I guess you're right," McCoy said gloomily.

"Nevertheless I agree that watching may be the only answer, and particularly by the ship's psychologist, meaning you, Doc. If there is a major personality reversal here, there's got to be something un-Spocklike to be seen in the replicate if we look hard enough for it."

"Any suggestions?"

"We'll have to play it by ear. But just for example, I'll tell you privately that I'm highly suspicious of Spock Two. The emotional pressure he has been bringing to bear on me to have the replicate destroyed is uncharacteristic. The conservative approach Spock One advocates seems more like the old Spock. But it's not enough to go on. We've *got* to have a test."

"Easy," McCoy said drily. "Just order Yeoman Rand to kiss one of them. If he responds shoot him."

"If we can't think of anything better, I'll do just that," Kirk said. "I'm dead serious, Doc."

"I know you are, Jim, and I'll keep my eyes peeled. Watching that human computer was a chore at the best of times, though. Having to watch two of them, under battle alert, is going to be a real cross."

Kirk left, temporarily satisfied. McCoy would follow the lead; it did not matter that he was sarcastic about it. He could no more avoid that than he could avoid breathing.

After the next day's watch—uneventful, but nerve-wracking—Kirk visited the engineering deck. Scott's report was no more encouraging than the surgeon's had been.

"I've been shooting out inanimate objects toward Organia's coordinates, Captain, and I've got quite a collection of duplicate mathoms th' noo. They don't tell us a thing we didna ken before."

"What's a mathom?"

"A useless object, alas. The things do replicate in reverse, so we can regard that hypothesis as confirmed. But I dinna see how that helps us. I suppose ye thought of checkin' the Spocks to see where they were wearin' their badges?"

"I did think of it, but not soon enough—not when the duplication first occurred. Now the replicate has had plenty of time to think of it himself and take steps."

"Well, an' next I'm goin' to send out an experimental animal an' give the replicate to Doc to play with. Though he won't see much in the way of personality reversal there. If it's a rabbit, maybe it'll bite him."

But the next day, all hopes for a testing program became academic—and in fact, impossible.

Spock Two was on the bridge when Kirk came on duty, to the Captain's rather disquieted surprise. He said at once, "Captain, I have issued no orders and would not be here at all were it not for the gravity of the situation. However, I must report that the entity you call Spock One has barricaded himself in Dr. McCoy's laboratory, and refuses to come out without a logged assurance of my destruction, and a guarantee of his own life."

The atmosphere on the bridge was like the inside of an electrostatic chamber. Kirk said, "Confirm!"

"Confirmed," the computer said.

Kirk snapped a glance at Uhura. "Lieutenant, ask Dr. McCoy to come up here, on the double. Mr. Spock, if you were he—that is, Spock One—what do you think you might be attempting to gain? Beyond, of course, trying to force my hand on the overt demands?"

"There are many possibilities, Captain. Simple disruption of ship's routine is one. Or trying to force a loyalty crisis among your other officers. Or an attempt to gain privacy in order to jury-rig some form of communication with the Klingons."

"Could you run up such a rig, in his circumstances?"

"Yes, in any of several different ways."

"Mr. Sulu, deflector screens up."

"Already up, Captain," the navigator said with indefatigable cheerfulness. At the same moment, McCoy entered.

"Doctor, is there anything in your laboratory that Spock One could adapt to damaging the ship—or the personnel?"

"Quite a lot," McCoy said. "In fact, probably more than I could guess. After all, he is the ship's science officer—or a more than reasonably accurate facsimile."

"Enough to justify our trying to cut our way in there with a phaser?"

"I would say not," McCoy said. "There's a lot of equipment in there that's irreplaceable under our present circumstances, to say nothing of a good many reagents and drugs. If he resisted, much of it could be damaged or destroyed—or he could stymie us by threatening to destroy it himself. And consider, Jim, that he may be doing nothing more than what he says he's doing: safeguarding his own life. Why not wait and see?"

"May I comment, Captain?" Spock Two said. Kirk nodded. "The risks in such a course are enormous. Surely this move—which is in direct violation of your standing orders to me—establishes that he is the replicate, not I. Leaving him unmolested is tantamount to inviting a highly qualified Klingon science officer aboard, handing him a full set of engineering tools and materials, and inviting him to do his worst."

"Think highly of yourself, don't you?" McCoy said.

"If you doubt that I am highly qualified, Doctor, I suggest that you ask the computer for my record."

"Cut it out, both of you," Kirk said. "This is no time for feuding. And Mr. Spock, I want you to bear in mind that I do not consider *anything* established as yet. I am highly suspicious of both of you, and the only chances I am prepared to take are those which will keep both of you alive. Dammit, man, don't you know that you're insisting on my destroying someone who may be my friend—as well as the best first officer in the Fleet? If you don't, then it's pretty clear that *you* can't be the original Spock!"

"Of course I understand it," Spock Two said. "But it is my duty to offer what I think to be the facts."

"It is," Kirk agreed, somewhat mollified. "However, for the present, we will leave this mess standing exactly as it is. In the meantime, I want you all to recall that we are still trying to dodge the Klingon navy and make a run for Organia—which is now our own best chance for survival, as well as of being of some use to the Federation."

"We may not be in time even at best, Captain," Lieutenant Uhura said. "I have just intercepted a general Klingon subspace broadcast. They claim to have inflicted a major defeat upon the Federation Fleet in the Great Nebula area of Orion. That's awfully close to Earth itself."

"It is more than that," Spock Two said. "It is the area which the Klingons call New Suns Space, because fourth-generation stars are being born there."

"Why does that matter?" Kirk said.

"Because, Captain, the process still has millions of years to run. It means that the Klingons are so confident of winning the war that they are willing to expend men and ships to capture solar systems that, as yet, do not even exist. And they may very well be right."

Chapter Six

NOBODY AT HOME

From the Captain's Log, Star Date 4150.0:

We are now three months deep into Klingon space and remain undetected, although we have overheard Klingon ships working out a search grid for us. Hence I have ruled against any smash-and-grab raids on Klingon bases, which might help them predict our course, until and unless the situation on Organia turns out to be hopeless. We also continue to hear reports of Federation defeats. The computer judges Spock Two's theory about the strange places in which the Klingon navy turns up to be highly probable, but there is still no way to report his conclusion to Starfleet Command. His behavior otherwise has been impeccable; but then, Spock One has been equally inoffensive, except for continuing to refuse to come out of his hole.

After three months, too, there was a spurious atmosphere of routine on the bridge, as though it were perfectly normal to have one Spock at the library console and one taking his meals behind a barricade in McCoy's laboratory. (An attempt to starve him out had come to nothing; he had, as he had promptly announced, simply put himself on iron rations from among McCoy's supplies—a diet which would have brought down any ordinary human being eventually with half a dozen deficiency diseases at once, but which could sustain his half-Vulcan constitution indefinitely.)

Kirk was just as well pleased to have his department heads adjusted to the situation. It was further evidence of their resiliency—not that he needed that, at this late date—and besides, nobody could afford to be distracted under present circumstances. McCoy and Scott, of course, continued to work doggedly at the problem of the replication whenever possible, but only one further clue had emerged: all of the experimental animals Scott had sent "out," in imitation of Spock's ill-fated non-journey, also "returned" as duplicates, but the duplicates all died within a few days thereafter. The surgeon could find no reason for their deaths, but even had he been able to do so, it seemed unlikely that the explanation would have been helpful, since it very obviously could not apply to the very much alive replicate Spock (whichever he was). Like all of the few other clues, it seemed to point nowhere in particular.

Gradually, however, the tension began to grow again as the *Enterprise* drew near to 11872 dy. by 85746 K, the arbitrary point in space-time where she would have to break out of warp drive in order to scan for Organia —and for something utterly unknown.

"Thus far," Kirk told his watch, "we've no reason to suppose that the Klingons think we're anywhere in the vicinity. But we'll take no chances. Mr. Sulu, I want you to engage ship's phasers with Lieutenant Uhura's sensor alarms, so that if we get a lock-on even the instant we come out of warp, we get a proximity explosion one nano-jiffy later. There's a faint chance that we may blow up a friend that way, but in this sector I think it can be discounted."

Sulu's hands flew over his board. Uhura watched hers like a cat, occasionally pouncing as she secured the sensor circuits to his navigation aids. The telltales for the phaser rooms came on, one after the other, as the hulking, deadly machines reached readiness.

"All primed, Captain," Sulu said.

"What is our breakout time?"

"Fourteen thirty-five twenty."

"Lieutenant Uhura, how long will you need for a minimum scan for Organia?"

"I can get one complete spherical atlas of the skies in ten seconds, Captain."

"Very well. Mr. Sulu, give us ten seconds in normal space, then turn to a heading of forty-eight Mark zero-six-nine at Warp One. Better set it into the computer, Mr. Spock."

Spock Two nodded, but Sulu asked, "Wouldn't it be easier to clock it from my board?"

"I want it both ways, as a fail-safe."

"Do you wish a countdown, Captain?" Spock Two said.

"I see no reason for it when we're on automatic. It just creates tension unnecessarily. Steady as you go, and stand by."

The minutes trickled away. Then, with the usual suddenness, the *Enterprise* was in normal space.

And with equal suddenness, nothing else was normal.

Though he could not tell how he sensed it, Kirk felt the presence of a huge maw, a wound, a vortex in the very fabric of space-time itself. It was as if some unimaginable force had torn open the underlying metrical frame of the universe, leaving absolute and utter Nothingness, the ultimate blankness which had preceded even the creation of Chaos. And the *Enterprise* was plunging straight into it.

The sensation was one of pure horror. Although the ten seconds seemed to stretch out into hours, Kirk was completely paralyzed, and around him his companions were as rigid as statues.

Then it was gone, as if it had never been. The *Enterprise* was back on Warp Drive.

The bell from the engineering deck jammered.

"What in bloody blue blazes was *thot?*"

"Don't know, Scotty, get off the blower till we figure it out and I'll pass you the word. I assume the rest of your crew felt it too?"

There was a brief silence. "Aye, that they did."

"Mr. Sulu, do we have our new heading?"

"Yes, *sir*," said the helmsman, white-lipped.

"Did you get your pictures, Lieutenant? Good, let's have a look at them. And open a line to Spock One—I have a hunch we're going to need all the brains we can muster to crack this nut."

The distorted stars of subspace vanished from the viewing screen, to be replaced by a normal-looking starfield. At its center, however, was a gently glowing, spherical object, fuzzy of appearance and with a peculiar silvery sheen.

"That," said Uhura, "is at the coordinates for Organia. Unless my own memory is playing me tricks, it hasn't the faintest resemblance to the images of Organia we have stored in the log from our first visit. Organia has pronounced surface markings and is a Class M planet. This thing looks like a gas giant, insofar as it looks like anything at all."

"In addition to the fact," Kirk said, "that we were heading straight for it when we came out of warp drive, and my mental and emotional impression was that there was nothing there at all—NOTHING in great quivering capital letters. Did anybody have a different impression?"

All shook their heads. Spock Two said, "Captain, we know the Organians are masters of hypnotism, and can manipulate other energy flows as well with great virtuosity. They are quite capable of giving their planet any apparent aspect that they like, even to the camera."

"In ten seconds?" Kirk said. "I'll grant that the emotional effect could be a part of some sort of general mental broadcast, but I doubt that even the Organians could jump aboard a ship and scramble its camera circuits that precisely on that short notice."

"Besides, my cameras aren't standard; I've rewired them a lot from time to time," Uhura said. "In order to know the circuits well enough to tinker with them, they'd have to read my mind, or get the altered wiring diagrams out of the computer."

"The full extent of their capabilities is quite un-known," Spock Two said.

"I'm not arguing about that," Kirk said. "But why should they give one impression to us and a quite different one to the cameras? Either they want us to think that Organia's not there, or that it has been drastically transformed—but why both? They know the contradiction would arouse our curiosity—though *both* appearances seem designed to discourage it, taken singly. And that seems to indicate that the camera appearance was not their work, and that the pictures show the real situation—whatever *that* is."

"If so," Spock Two said, "it is logically economical to suppose that there is a common explanation: that the Organians have surrounded their planet with some kind of an energy screen, which is what the cameras see, and whose effects are what we felt."

"That's reasonable," Kirk said. "But if true, it throws a large wooden shoe into our original plan. To put it mildly, I have the distinct feeling that the Organians do *not* want to be visited. And if we were to go down there anyhow, I'm sure I wouldn't be able to stand up under the pressure of that field for more than a minute. Do I hear any volunteers who think they might?"

Nobody volunteered. At length Kirk said, "Spock One, we've heard nothing from you thus far. Have you any thoughts on this problem?"

"Yes, Captain," the intercom said in Spock's voice. "Though I have not seen the pictures in question, your discussions have been complete enough to permit analysis. It seems evident that you are all off on the wrong track. The answer is in fact quite simple, though far from obvious."

"All right, what is it? Spit it out, man."

"Only on receipt of my guarantees, Captain."

"That," Kirk said grimly, "is blackmail."

"The term is accurate, and therefore neither offends nor persuades me."

"And what about the security of the ship?"

"My analysis of the situation," the intercom said,

"leads me to conclude that the presence of the replicate first officer is a greater danger to the security of the ship than is the inaccessibility of Organia. I therefore continue to insist upon my terms."

Kirk turned angrily to the simulacrum of the first officer who was on the bridge. "Spock Two, do you have any idea of what he might be hinting at?"

"None whatsoever, I regret to say. Our thought processes are now markedly different, as I predicted from the start that they would become. From the data available, I believe your present view of the Organian situation to be the correct one, though necessarily incomplete."

That was superficially reassuring, Kirk thought, but actually no help at all. If Spock One did indeed have the answer, it might be worth giving him the guarantees he demanded (what was it that Shylock kept saying in *The Merchant of Venice?* "I'll have my bond!") to get it—which Spock Two, especially if he was the replicate, would resist to protect his own life. But if Spock One was the replicate, his claim to have a solution might simple be a ruse to insure the destruction of the original. If his solution turned out to be wrong, well, he could always plead inadequate data; Kirk had never required his first officer to be infallible, much though Spock himself disliked finding himself in error.

"We'll proceed on our present assumption," Kirk said finally. "Working from those, the only chance we have of rescuing any part of our original plan is to find some way of getting past that screen, shielding ourselves from its effects, or neutralizing it entirely. I'll throw that little gem to Mr. Scott, but he'll have to have detailed sensor readings from the screen to analyze—which, I'm sorry to say, means another pass through the sector off warp drive. Orders:

"Lieutenant Uhura, find out from Mr. Scott what sensor setup he thinks would be most likely to be helpful to him, and what is the shortest possible time in which he could get sufficient readings. And once Mr. Sulu has set up a flight plan for the pass, make sure the

entire crew is forewarned to expect another one of those
emotional shocks, and how long it will last.

"Spock Two, have the computer print out a complete
rundown of anything that might be known about any
screen even vaguely like this one—including conjec-
tures—and turn it over to Mr. Scott." He stood up
tiredly. "I'm going to the rec room for a sandwich. If
I'm not back by the time the pass is set up, call me.
All other arrangements for the pass are to be as they
were before."

"You are making a serious mistake, Captain," said
the voice of Spock One.

"You leave me no choice, Mr. Spock. All hands,
execute!"

Kirk was more or less braced for the impact of the
terror when the next moment of breakout came, but the
preparation did not seem to do him much good. The
experience was in fact worse this time, for it had to be
longer—Scott had insisted upon a run of forty-five
interminable seconds, during which the *Enterprise* and
all her crew seemed to be falling straight into the Pit.
And during the last ten seconds, there was a flash of
intense white flame off to one side—the burst of a
proximity explosion from one of the ship's phasers.
Three seconds later, there was still another.

"Heels, Sulu!" Uhura cried. "The place is swarming
with Klingons!"

Chapter Seven

THE ATTACK

From the Captain's Log, Star Date 4181.6:

Apparently six Klingon battlecraft locked onto us during our second pass at Organia—or whatever it is where Organia ought to be. If they were in the vicinity during our first pass, which I think almost certain, only the briefness of our breakout can have saved us from being detected then. It is also possible, of course, that we would not have been detected the second time had it not been for our own automatic phaser fire, depending upon whether the Klingon force was a garrison or an ambush. If it was the latter, the proximity setting on the phasers did us a favor, for our hits must have disabled two of them; only four are following on warp drive. With another enemy I would expect someone to stay behind as a reserve, out of ordinary tactical common sense, but no Klingon would avoid a fight unless physically pinned down in one way or another.

Most battles in space are either over almost the instant they begin—as had evidently been the case with the two surprised Klingon vessels—or became very protracted affairs, because of the immense distances involved. (The first sentence of Starfleet Academy's *Fundamentals of Naval Engagement* reads: "The chief obstacle facing a Starship Captain who wishes to join battle is that battle is almost impossible to join.")

This one showed every sign of going on forever. None

of the four surviving Klingon ships was as large as their quarry, whose phasers outranged theirs sufficiently to keep them at a respectful distance, while her deflectors easily swept aside the occasional Klingon torpedo. In short, a standoff.

Kirk knew from experience, however, that the standoff could not be a stalemate; the blasts of code being emitted steadily on subspace radio by the small Klingon vessels—three of them seemed to be corvettes, the other was perhaps as large as a cruiser—were obviously urgent calls for more high-powered help. Nor was there any further reason for the *Enterprise* to preserve radio silence.

"Inform Starfleet Command of our whereabouts," he told Lieutenant Uhura. "Include a description of the Organian situation and a hologram of your best plate of the body in Organia's orbit. Tell them we're under attack and ask for orders. Second, as a separate message, send them Spock Two's conclusions on current Klingon strategy. Third, route a flash Urgent straight through to the Scientific Advisory Board describing our superfluity of Spocks and exactly how it happened—with hard, *full* particulars from Mr. Scott—and ask them for analysis and advice . . . By the way, how old is our most recent code?"

"Just a year old, Captain."

"The Klingons will have broken that six ways from Sunday by now. Well, you'll have to use it—but put the clear in Swahili and ask to get the answers the same way. That ought to give the Klingons pause."

"It will indeed," Uhura said, grinning. "But even modern Swahili lacks some of Scotty's technical terms, Captain. There are Indo-European borrowings in every Earthly language—and the Klingons may be able to infer the rest of the message using them as contexts."

"Blast and damn. Leaving the technicalities out will throw us right back on our own resources, and I can't say we've done too well with those."

"There's an alternative, Captain, though it's risky; we can translate the clear into Eurish."

"What's that? I never heard of it."

"It's the synthetic language James Joyce invented for his last novel, over two hundred years ago. It contains forty or fifty other languages, including slang in all of them. Nobody but an Earthman could possibly make sense of it, and there are only a few hundred of them who are fluent in it. There's the risk; it may take Starfleet Command some time to run down an expert in it—if they even recognize it for what it is."

Being a communications officer, Kirk realized anew, involved a good many fields of knowledge besides subspace radio. "Can it handle scientific terms?"

"Indeed it can. You know the elementary particle called the quark; well, that's a Eurish word. Joyce himself predicted nuclear fission in the novel I mentioned. I can't quote it precisely, but roughly it goes, 'The abnihilisation of the etym expolodotonates through Parsuralia with an ivanmorinthorrorumble fragorom-boassity amidwhiches general uttermosts confussion are perceivable moletons skaping with mulicules.' There's more, but I can't recall it—it has been a long time since I last read the book."

"That's more than enough," Kirk said hastily. "Go ahead—just as long as you're sure you can read the answer."

"Nobody's ever *dead* sure of what Eurish means," Uhura said. "But I can probably read more of it than the Kligons could. To them, it'll be pure gibberish."

And they won't be alone, Kirk thought. Nevertheless, he could forget about it for the time being. That still left the problem of the Klingon ships on the tail of the *Enterprise*.

Sowing a mine field in the ship's wake would be useless; the enemy craft doubtless had deflectors, and in any event the mines, being too small to carry their own warp generators, would simply fall out into normal space and become a hazard to peacetime navigation. But wait a minute . . .

"Mr. Spock, check me on something. When we put out a deflector beam when we're on warp drive, the warp field flows along the beam to the limit of the surface area of the field. Then, theoretically, the field fails and we're back in normal space. All right so far?"

"Yes, Captain, a simple inverse-square-law effect."

"And contrariwise," Kirk said, "using a tractor beam on warp drive pulls the field in around the beam, which gives us a little extra velocity but dangerously biases our heading." Spock Two nodded. "All right, I think we've got the basis for a little experiment. I want to plant a mine right under the bow of that cruiser, using a deflector *and* a tractor beam in tandem, with a little more power on the deflector. At the same time, I want our velocity run up so that our warp field will fail just as the mine explodes. Fill in the parameters, including the cruiser's pseudo distance and relative velocity, and see if it's feasible."

Spock Two turned to the computer and worked silently for a few moments. Then he said, "Yes, Captain, mathematically it is not a complex operation. But the library has no record of any Starship ever surviving the puncturing of its warp field by a deflector while under drive."

"And when nearly balanced by a tractor?"

"No pertinent data. At best, I would estimate, the strain on the *Enterprise* would be severe."

Yes, Kirk thought, and just maybe you don't much want that Klingon cruiser knocked out, either.

"We'll try it anyhow. Mr. Sulu, arm a mine and program the operation. Also—the instant we are back in normal space, give us maximum acceleration along our present heading on reaction drive."

"That," Spock Two said in the original Spock's most neutral voice, "involves a high probability of shearing the command section free of the engineering section."

"Why? We've done it before."

"Because of the compounding of the shock incident upon the puncturing of the warp field, Captain."

"We'll take that chance too. In case it has escaped your attention, we happen to be in the middle of a battle. Lieutenant, warn ship's personnel to beware shock. Stand to, all, and execute."

Spock Two offered no further obstructions. Silently, Uhura set up on the main viewing screen a panorama of the sector in which the trap—if it worked—was to be sprung. The Klingon cruiser would have looked like a distorted mass of tubes and bulbs even close on, under the strange conditions of subspace; at its present distance, it was little more than a wobbly shadow.

Then the dense, irregular mass, made fuzzy with interference fringes, which was the best view they could hope to get of the mine, pushed its way onto the screen, held at the tip of two feathers of pale light, their pinnae pointing in opposite directions, which were the paired deflector and tractor beams (which in normal space would have been invisible). As the mine reached the inside surface of the warp field, that too became faintly visible, and in a moment was bulging toward the Klingon vessel. The impression it gave, of a monstrous balloon about to have a blowout, was alarming.

"Mr. Sulu, can the Klingon see what's going on there from the outside, or otherwise sense it?"

"I don't know, Captain. I wish *I* couldn't."

"Lieutenant Uhura?"

"It's quite possible, Captain, considering how excited the warp field is becoming. But perhaps they won't know how to interpret it. Like the library, I've never heard of this having been tried before, and maybe the Klingons haven't either. But I'm only guessing."

The bulge in the warp field grew, gradually becoming a blunt pseudopod groping into subspace. From the *Enterprise* it was like staring down a dim tunnel, with the twin beams as its axis. From the depths of his memory there came to Kirk a biology-class vision of the long glass spike of a radiolarian, a microscopic marine animal, with protoplasm streaming along it, mindless and voracious.

"Captain," the intercom squawked. "I've got trouble down here already. My engines are croonin' like kine with the indigestion."

"Ride with it, Mr. Scott, there's worse to come."

The blunt projection became a finger, at the tip of which the mine, looking as harmless as a laburnum seed, dwindled into the false night of subspace. Very faintly, the hull of the *Enterprise* began to groan. It was the first time in years that Kirk had heard his ship betray any signs of structural strain serious enough to be audible.

"Thirty seconds to breakout," Spock Two said.

"The Klingon's peeling off!" Uhura cried. "He's detected *something* he doesn't like, that's for sure. And he's under full drive. If . . ."

Was the mine close enough? Never mind, it would never be any closer.

"Fire, Mr. Sulu," Kirk said.

An immense ball of flame blossomed on the view screen—and then vanished as the *Enterprise* dropped into normal space. One second later, deprived of the ship's warp field, the fireball, too, was back again.

"Got him!" Sulu crowed.

The fireball swelled intolerably as the matter and anti-matter in the doomed Klingon's warp-drive pods fused and added their violence to the raging hydrogen explosion of the mine. The viewing screen dimmed the light hurriedly, but finally could accomodate it no longer, and blacked out entirely.

At the same time, the *Enterprise* rang with the blow-torch howling of the reaction engines coming up to full thrust, and a colossal lurch threw them all to the deck. The light flickered.

"Posts!" Kirk shouted, scrambling back to his command chair. "All department heads, report!"

The ship was screaming so fearfully in all its members that he could not have heard the answers even had his staff been able to hear the order. But a sweeping glance over the boards told him the bare-knuckle essentials; the rest could wait though not for long.

The *Enterprise* had held together—just barely. The three surviving Klingon corvettes had taken several seconds to react to the destruction of their command cruiser and the disappearance of their quarry. They had dropped out of warp drive now, but in those few seconds had overshot their target by nearly a million miles, and the long, separating arcs they were executing now to retrace their steps were eloquent of caution and bafflement—and, if Kirk knew his Klingons, of mind-clouding fury.

The *Enterprise,* so fleet on warp drive, was something of a pig under reaction thrust, but she was wallowing forward bravely, and gaining legs with every stride. Within only a few minutes she would be plowing through the very midst of her erstwhile harriers.

"Klingons launching missiles, Captain," Uhura reported.

Pure, random desperation. "Disregard. Mr. Sulu, engage the enemy and fire at will. When you're through with them, I don't want one single atom left sticking to another."

"Yes, *sir,*" Sulu said, a wolfish grin on his normally cheerful face. This was the opportunity of a lifetime for a Starship gunnery officer, and he was obviously enjoying it thoroughly.

As the *Enterprise* picked up speed, she responded better to her helm; in that respect she did not differ much from a nineteenth-century clipper ship on the high seas, though the comparison failed utterly on warp drive. And she had a tremendous amount of energy to expand—indeed, even to waste—through her reaction engines. The Klingons apparently were stunned to see her bearing down on them, but their stupor didn't matter now. The corvettes could not have reformed in time to meet her, even had their commanders understood the situation instantly.

Sulu's hands danced over the studs before him. A stabbing barrage of phaser fire shot out from the *Enterprise.* The deflector screens of the corvettes fought back with coruscating brilliance; the viewing screen, which had crept cautiously back into operation after the death of the cruiser, dimmed hastily again.

Then there were no Klingon corvettes—only clouds

of incandescent gas, through which the *Enterprise* sailed as majestically as an ancient Spanish galleon over a placid Caribbean bay.

"Very good, ladies and gentlemen," Kirk said. "Assess damage and report to the First Officer. Mr. Sulu, re-lay course for Organia at Warp Three, to a position in opposition to the present calculated position of the planet. Lieutenant Uhura, open all lines to the staff—including Spock One. I want a conference, as of right now."

"I'll give you a report, Captain Kirk, and it's a twenty-four carat dilly," Leonard McCoy's voice said out of the middle of the air. "I can now tell you *how to determine which Spock is the ringer.*"

Kirk shot a glance at Spock Two, but the incumbent First Officer showed no reaction whatsoever. Well, that was in character, as far as it went; Kirk had expected nothing else.

"Belay that," Kirk told McCoy evenly. "Our present business is much more urgent, and I want *both* Spocks to hear it."

"But, Jim—!" McCoy's voice said, almost as if in shock. Then there was a sound of swallowing, and the surgeon started over again. "Captain, this matter in my opinion has the highest possible urgency."

"Belay it. And attend, all."

Chapter Eight

SPOCKS ON TRIAL

From the Captain's Log, Star Date 4194.4:

Despite Spock Two's alarming predictions, the damage to the ship from the maneuver of this morning appears to be minimal, consisting chiefly of a deflector generator failure and some even less important burnouts of scattered sensor units. All of this is easily reparable from ship's stores, Mr. Scott reports. In the meantime, there appear to be no Klingon vessels in or near this arc of Organia's orbit, and I mean to use the breather this affords us to bring several other matters to a head—and high time, too.

Those sensors that were still alive—a large majority—were at full extension and tied in to an automatic flight plan; the bridge staff were at their consoles; and lines were open to the engineering bridge, to the sick bay, to McCoy's laboratory, and to the transporter room. Kirk looked at each of his physically present department chiefs in turn, and his expression was glacial.

"We have been acting first, and thinking afterward, entirely too much," he said, "and I do not except myself. Nor am I blaming anyone, since we've been under continuous pressure, both of emotion and of event. But it's time for a casting up of accounts.

"First of all, I find that Klingon reception committee highly peculiar. There are two ways of regarding it, as far as I can see:

"One: that it was a trap that had been set for us. This implies advance knowledge of where we were going to be, and I think it's safe to say that the Klingons couldn't have come by such knowledge unless somebody aboard the *Enterprise* got it to them, somehow.

"Two: that the Klingon force was stationed in this area anyhow, and jumped us as a matter of course when we showed up. The main difficulty with that theory is that it requires another one, and I'm no fonder of *ad hoc* assumptions than Mr. Spock is. Why should the Klingons post five ships—a cruiser, three corvettes and a fifth ship of unknown size—so far from the main battle area? We already know that their forces are penetrating deeply, and with great daring, into Federation space. If those five ships were simply part of a reserve, why were they stationed here, a good long way away from any Klingon base big enough to supply them, and so far away from Federation territory that they couldn't have been thrown into any battle fast enough to reinforce a Klingon fleet in trouble? That's utterly uncharacteristic of them, and it doesn't make sense any other way, either."

There was dead silence. Kirk let his expression soften a little, and added, "Anyone who wishes to volunteer an opinion is at liberty to do so."

"In that case, Captain, I have a third hypothesis to suggest," said the voice of Spock One.

"With no price tag?"

"None, Captain. I ask for my price only on what I *know* to be the case. At present, what I have to offer is only a possible alternative to your theories. It is this:

"The Klingons may well have invested the Organian system because they regard it as a sensitive area. They may no more understand what has happened to the planet than we do; but they certainly know that should the Organians choose to come back from wherever they have gone, or whatever state or condition they may be in, the war would be over. And worse; since the Klingons started the war in defiance of the Organian

Peace Treaty, their return would place the Klingons, as an old Earth expression has it, in the soup."

"No possible or even imaginable Klingon naval force could prevent the Organians from taking action if they chose to do so," Spock Two said, "and it is elementary games theory to assume that the Klingons know this."

"Quite true," said the voice of Spock One. "But if they do *not* understand what has happened to Organia—contrary to my original assumption that they might have *caused* it—they would not want any Federation ship investigating the situation and possibly finding out the answer before they did, especially not a vessel as well equipped for research as a Starship. They would infinitely prefer the *status quo;* and so, they deploy valuable forces around the area."

Despite the fact that the presence of the two Spocks aboard the *Enterprise* was now one hundred and seventy-six days old, it still gave Kirk a faint chill to listen to the two identical voices arguing with each other, as if he were deep in some nightmare from which he was never going to awaken. The dispassionate tone of both voices, as they pursued a discussion which must end, eventually, in the death of one of them, made it even more eerie. With an effort, he said, "Spock One, six weeks ago you were claiming positive knowledge of what had happened to Organia. Now you've changed your tune."

"Not at all, Captain. I do know what has happened to Organia. I simply offer an alternate hypothesis as to its cause, and the Klingons' response."

"Spock Two, what's your opinion of this hypothesis?"

"It has certain attractive features," Spock Two said. "For instance, it explains why the Klingons did not attack us when we first appeared in the area. Had they had a trap prepared, they would have blown us out of space within a few seconds; they are highly efficient in such matters, as the Captain will recall. Whereas, as a garrison force, they would have been taken by surprise by our first irruption."

"And another 'attractive feature,'" Kirk said stonily,

"is that the theory doesn't require the ship to have been betrayed—by either one of you."

"May I butt in, Captain?" Sulu said.

"Go right ahead, Mr. Sulu."

"There exists no way whatsoever by which the Klingons could have known we were coming here. They couldn't possibly have predicted my course after we shook that first little craft. And in normal space, they couldn't have detected our approach in warp drive either, isn't that right, Uhura?"

"Out of the question," the communications officer agreed.

"So," Sulu said, "a garrison seems to be the answer."

"It sounds plausible," Kirk said, "but unless I read the signs wrong, Spock Two has some reservations. What are they?"

"I would not describe them as reservations, Captain. I have myself suddenly realized what happened to Organia. The answer also contains the solution of the duplication problem, as was almost inevitable. Hence there is no further need for us to trade in guesses and probabilities. I should add, however, that the solution absolutely requires the destruction of the replicate in Dr. McCoy's laboratory."

"Why?" Kirk said, in rising desperation.

"Because he also claims to know the answer. I cannot say for certain whether his answer is the same as mine. I hope it is not. It is vital that he not have the correct answer, or, if he does have it, that he not be allowed to act on it."

"So you're holding out on me too, eh?"

"I regret that I must," Spock Two said.

"I am getting so damn tired of all this blackmail," Kirk said, "that I'm more than tempted to get rid of you *both*. Never mind, forget that I said it. Mr. Scott."

"Aye, Captain."

"Does anything you've heard this time offer you any clues to your side of the problem?"

"It makes nae physical sense to me at all, Captain, I'm verra sorry to say."

"Dr. McCoy, what about your method for distinguishing between the two Spocks? Does that have any bearing on the other questions?"

"It probably does, Captain, but if so I don't see how. I'm nevertheless quite sure of it, on biological grounds alone. In fact I'm so sure, that I can tell you right now which one is the replicate, and I will, and I *won't* put any price on the information, either. It has to be Spock One."

"But you can't tell me which of the two has the right answer to the problem of Organia—or even how the replication itself happened?"

"Sorry, Jim, but I haven't the foggiest notion."

"Then we're still up in the air. Both Spocks claim to have those answers, and neither one will tell me what they are. We have to keep both men with us until we find out what they're concealing—or if, on the other hand, they're both of them simply bluffing."

"One of us," Spock One said, "is the original and therefore cannot be bluffing, Captain. Surely you will do him that courtesy."

Kirk put a hand briefly over his eyes. "I'll offer an apology to the survivor. And I'll assume that one of you is telling the truth, of course. *But which?* The honest man, the real Spock, ought to offer his information freely; that's his duty. Yet you're both insisting, now, upon the death of the other Spock before you'll talk. This is more than blackmail—it's an endorsement of murder. That's enough to make me wonder if *either* of you can be the original Spock."

Now *there* was a nasty notion. Suppose the original had been destroyed in the mysterious accident in the transporter room, and both of these were replicates? But McCoy thought otherwise. Kirk was glad the idea hadn't occurred to him earlier.

The rest of the staff on the bridge was listening with breathless fascination, as if they were onlookers at a performance of the penultimate act of a tragedy—as indeed they might be.

"May I point out, Captain, as you did during the

battle, that we are at war?" said Spock Two. "To my certain knowledge, the replicate Spock must be, and is, a creature of the enemy, exactly as I proposed to you when you confronted the two of us in my quarters, nearly six months ago. The wages of treason are death for a good reason, Captain: not as a punishment, for we know capital punishment is useless as a deterrent, but because the traitor belongs *by conviction* to the enemy, and is therefore a permanent danger as long as the enemy himself remains an enemy."

"And what about due process of law?" Kirk said. "You're asking me for the death of Spock One, as far as I can see, as if it were a marketplace transaction—his death in exchange for your information, just as though you were a quartermaster charging me for a uniform. It's a man's life we're dealing with here, and I'm not about to condemn him to death, even for treason, without trial and conviction."

"To what tribunal could we submit such a case?" said the voice of Spock One. "There is no competent community of appeal aboard the *Enterprise*."

"You can appeal it to me," McCoy said, in a voice that sounded as if it was full of gravel. "*I* can tell the two of you apart, I know I'm right, and it's easy to put to the test. Do you want to hear my proposal privately, Jim, or shall I just blurt it right out?"

"The accused have a right to know how they'll be tried. Speak up, Doc, it's getting late. There may be Klingons on our backs again any minute."

"Very good, Captain. The test is this: let the barricaded Spock out, if he'll come, and offer both men a standard ship's meal. One of them will refuse it. That man is the ringer—and very likely a traitor too, at least potentially."

Kirk leaned back in his command chair, feeling his jaw dropping. Were all these high issues, all these personal conflicts, all these emotional and military tensions to be resolved with two plates of chicken-and-quadrotriticale soup? It was a fantastic anticlimax; for an instant, he felt that he would almost rather have the problem than this answer. But he said finally, "Do you really think this is a critical test, Doc?"

"Yes, I do, Captain. If it fails, you're no worse off than before. But I assure you, it won't fail."

Kirk turned to the incumbent First Officer.

"Spock Two, do you agree?"

"I do," Spock Two said promptly. "Since I've been eating standard ship's fare for months within everybody's observation anyhow. And may I add, Captain, that the test is a highly elegant, simple and ingenious one. I congratulate Dr. McCoy; it had not occurred to me at all."

"Spock One, do you also agree to it?"

There was no answer.

"Spock One, I'll give you just ten seconds to reply."

No answer. The seconds ran out.

"Security! Two guards to the bridge, please. Three more to Dr. McCoy's laboratory on the double and burn through the door. Capture the man inside alive if possible. If not possible, defend yourselves to the limit."

Spock Two turned in his chair as if to stand up. Instantly, Kirk's very small personal phaser was in his hand and leveled at Spock Two's stomach. Kirk had not had ancestors in America's Far West for nothing; he had practiced that draw endlessly in the ship's gymnasium, and this was not the first time he had been glad that he'd kept at it.

"Remain seated, my friend," he said, "until the security guards get here. And I devoutly hope that you really are my friend. But until I'm absolutely certain that you are, I'm quite willing to stun you so thoroughly that you won't wake up until next Easter—or maybe, never. Do I make myself clear?"

"Quite clear, Captain," Spock Two said composedly. "An entirely logical precaution."

Chapter Nine

THE MAN IN THE MIRROR

From the Captain's Log, Star Date 4194.6:

Whenever Spock One took alarm, he seems to have left himself plenty of time; he was gone by the time we cut our way into McCoy's laboratory, evidently out the ventilator shaft. There was no damage to the lab equipment other than that we caused ourselves by breaking in, but Spock One had set up a complex maze of tubing and glassware in which various fluids were still bubbling, percolating and dripping. An ion exchange column and a counter-current distributor were the only parts of this rig that I recognized. I have forbidden anyone to touch it until McCoy can study it, but he says he thinks he already knows its purpose.

In the meantime, conducting any sort of major search for Spock One is out of the question. He knows every cubic centimeter of the ship, including the huge maze of the 'tween-hulls area, better than anyone else aboard except Scott, and hence could be anywhere by now. I have posted one guard over Spock Two in his quarters, another over myself and each of the department heads and their alternates, and several in the transporter room, the hangar deck, the passenger quarters (a prime target because currently empty), the engineering deck, the rec room, the main bridge, the briefing room, the gymnasium, the quartermaster's stores and the armory, as well as the laboratory, and if I have missed anyplace crucial where he might turn up, there is nothing I can do about it—I have used up everyone I can possibly assign to security duty without dangerously depleting the fighting and operating strength of the *Enterprise*.

I have ordered six hours' sleep for everyone who was on duty during the battle and have named Mr. Chekov Officer of the Day. I shall get some sleep myself when he comes onto the bridge. In the meantime, I have an interview with Dr. McCoy in ten minutes.

"The apparatus in the laboratory completely confirms my guesses about the situation," McCoy said, "which means that you can let Spock Two out now. He's the real thing, all right."

"What was it? The apparatus, I mean?"

"A system for synthesizing his own food, using the ship's meals we sent him as raw material, plus some of my reagents. That's why he chose my lab to barricade himself in—in addition, of course, to the chance it offered to hold all my equipment hostage. He could have holed up anyplace in order to avoid eating with the rest of us, but there was no place else aboard where he could have been his own chef."

Kirk was completely baffled. The explanation was no better than none at all.

"?" he said with his eyebrows.

"All right, I'll begin at the beginning," McCoy said. "Although it's hard to decide just what the beginning is. You'll remember that Spock Two suggested that the replicate might be a mirror image of the original, and later, you and I discussed the possibility."

"And could figure out no way to test it."

"Right. Well, subsequently Scotty supplied me with some experimental animals which he had put through the new transporter system, and there was no doubt about it—the replicates of those *were* mirror images. They seemed quite healthy otherwise, with lively appetites—but they all died within a day or so, as I reported to you.

"I did autopsies on them, of course, but the only conclusion I could come to was that they had died of starvation, despite the fact that they had all been chomping their way through the chow just as steadily as vegetarian animals like rabbits have to do to stay alive. I didn't understand this at all. And worse, it seemed to have no application to the problem of the two Spocks. Whichever of those was the replicate, he *wasn't* starving.

"It makes me feel pretty stupid to remember that I didn't grasp the clue even after Spock One shut himself up in my laboratory. What did finally give me the key was something that happened almost at the beginning of this affair—something apparently meaningless and irrelevant. It was this: You told me, you'll recall, that in your very first private interview with Spock One, he showed a slight hesitation in his speech, almost like stuttering."

Kirk thought back. "Yes, that's true, Doc. But it vanished almost immediately. I thought I might have imagined it."

"You didn't. Only someone with the iron control of a Spock could have made it vanish over any period of time, but his letting it show at all was his Achilles heel. As the replicate, and a mirror image, he was left-handed, just as we had guessed, but he was suppressing it, as we had also guessed. Now, Jim, handedness is the major physical expression of which hemisphere of a man's brain is the dominant one, the one chiefly in charge of his actions. It's a transverse relationship; if the left hemisphere of your brain is dominant, as is usually the case, you will be right-handed—and vice versa. And so, Jim, the retraining of left-handed children to become right-handed—in complete contradiction to the orders the poor kids' brains are issuing to their muscles—badly bollixes up their central nervous systems, and, among other bad outcomes, is the direct *and only* cause of habitual stuttering. You thought Spock One was stuttering from emotion or confusion, and that puzzled you. And well it might have. But in fact, he was stuttering because he was counterfeiting *not* being a mirror image, and hadn't gotten all his reflexes for the impersonation established yet."

"A brilliant piece of deduction, Mr. Holmes," Kirk said. "But I still don't see the connection between all that, and the food business."

"Because I haven't come to it yet. Let's backtrack for a minute. I don't have to explain to you how important the amino acids are to animal nutrition— they are the building blocks of protein. But what you may not know is that each amino acid has two molecular forms. If you crystallize a pure amino, aspargine for instance, and pass a beam of polarized light through the crystal, the beam will be bent when it emerges, either to the left or to the right. It's the levulo-rotatory form, the one that bends the beam to the left, that the body needs; the dextro-rotatory form is useless.

"And evidently the mirror-reversal of Spock One went all the way down to the molecular level of his being. Those nutrients we have to have, he cannot use; and those that he must have, he can't get from our food.

"There may be even more to it than that. It was not only starvation that he faced—no matter how much he ate, like my rabbits—but also the possibility that his central nervous system might be poisoned if he ate our food. For obvious reasons, no human being has ever tried to live on a diet consisting exclusively of reversed aminos, so nobody knows whether they might be subtly toxic to the higher brain functions—the functions that animals don't have. Obviously, Spock One didn't want to take any chances on that. He simply fasted for the few days he needed to contrive a good excuse for barricading himself in the lab. As a Vulcan hybrid he could go without food that long quite easily, and he did it so subtly that even Christine didn't notice that he wasn't eating. And then . . ."

"And then he set himself up to synthesize all twenty-eight amino acids for himself, and in bulk," Kirk said. "In a word—whew!"

"No, that would be beyond even a Spock, any Spock; my lab didn't have the facilities for it. But luckily for him, only eight of the aminos are absolutely essential in the diet. The rest can be synthesized by the body itself, from simpler raw materials. But even doing that much for himself was a pretty impressive achievement, I must admit."

"And he hasn't shot his bolt yet, either. Well, Doc, make sure you report this in full to Scotty."

"Oh," the surgeon said, "I already have it on tape for him. I was only delaying transmission until I'd gotten your reaction."

"Very good; you have that. Now—any guesses as to where Spock One might have holed up?"

"Not the slightest. His psychology must be completely reversed, too, and I never did understand that when it was going in what I laughingly called its normal direction."

Kirk grinned tiredly. "You've pulled off a miracle already," he said. "I can't very well ask for two in the same day. Congratulations, Doc."

"Many thanks. What are you going to do now, Jim, if I may ask?"

"I," Kirk said, "am going to my quarters and get some shut-eye. I think the *Enterprise* will be better off for a while if I'm asleep on my back—instead of on my feet."

"I'm glad to hear you say so," McCoy said soberly. "Otherwise I was going to tell you that myself—and damn well make it stick, too."

Kirk had had perhaps three hours' sleep—certainly no more—when the general alarm brought him bolt upright in his bunk.

"Mr. Chekov!" he snapped. "What's up?"

"Spock One, Captain," said the intercom. "He has just been spotted in the stores deck, very briefly. I've ordered all available security hands to converge on the area."

"Cancel that," Kirk said, coming fully awake for what seemed to him to be the first time in weeks. "Use only security hands in the engineering section proper; order full viewer scan of stores and monitor it from the bridge. All other security details to remain at their posts. Lock all stores exits with new codes."

"Right. Will you be assuming the bridge, Captain?"

"Directly."

But Spock One had obviously chosen his striking hour with great care, and his timing was perfect. Evidently his fleeting appearance in the stores area had been only a feint, for the search of stores had just gotten into full swing when the main board on the bridge signaled that the huge exit doors to the hangar deck—the doubled doors that led into space at the rear of the ship—were being rolled open, on manual override. Before the override could be interdicted from the bridge, the doors had parted enough to allow a shuttlecraft to get out, and flick away at top acceleration into the glare of the Organian sun.

"Tractors!" Kirk snapped.

"Sorry, Captain," Chekov said. "He has just gone into warp drive."

We have no shuttlecraft with warp drive, Kirk thought grayly; and then, *Well, we do now.*

"And good riddance," said McCoy, who had arrived on the bridge just in time to see the end of the fiasco.

"Do you really think we're rid of him, Doctor?" Kirk said icily. "I think that nothing could be more unlikely."

"And so," said Spock Two, "do I."

"Communications, track that shuttlecraft and monitor for any attempt on its part to get in touch with the Klingons. If it tries within range, jam it. Helmsman, put a homing missile on its tail, but don't arm its warhead until further orders. All security forces, resume search of the *Enterprise* as before, and this time include the interiors of all remaining shuttlecraft. Mr. Spock, attempt to gain remote control of the runaway shuttle and return it to the ship—but if you do get it back, *don't let it in.*"

He paused for a moment to let the orders sink in, along with their implications. Then he added, "This has been a fearfully lax operation on everyone's part, not excluding my own, and from now on it is going to be taut. Does everyone understand that?"

Though there were no answers, it was clear that everyone did.

Chapter Ten

A SCOTCH VERDICT

From the Captain's Log, Star Date 4196.2:

Hindsight is seldom a useful commodity, as all history seems to show; but it now seems almost inevitable, all the same, that Spock One should have chosen the hangar deck as his second hiding place. Not only is the area as big as a college playing field, and relatively poorly lit even when in use, but we almost never have any need for a shuttlecraft which can't be filled better and faster by the transporter. Furthermore, even so small a ship as a seven-man reaction-drive shuttle offers abundant crannies in which to hole up, plus drinking water supplies (and Dr. McCoy tells me that Spock One could safely eat the carbohydrates from the shuttle's food stores, too, since carbohydrates don't have alternate molecular forms); and we have (or had) six such craft—*not one of which* we could scan inside from the main bridge, visually or with any other sensor, except for its control room and its power storage level. But none of this occurred to any of us until too late. Having a Spock for an enemy is a supernally dangerous situation.

In the meantime, our tracking missile's trace seems to show that Spock One, if he is in fact aboard the runaway shuttlecraft, is heading straight for what used to be Organia, for reasons we can only guess at. Another mystery is how Spock One managed to convert the shuttlecraft's engines to warp drive in so short a time, and without a supply of anti-matter or any way of handling it. But this is a puzzle for Mr. Scott; it may some day be a matter of vast importance for Federation technology, but under present circumstances I judge it distinctly minor.

"I've got an answer, Captain," Scott said.

He was in Kirk's quarters, together with Dr. McCoy and the remaining first officer. The *Enterprise* was still in Organia's orbit, on the opposite side of Organia's star from what had used to be the planet. She was still on full battle alert; no new Klingon ships had showed up yet, but their arrival could not be long delayed—and this time, Kirk expected at least one Star Class battleship to be among them. Against such a force, the *Enterprise* could put up a brave fight, but the outcome was foreordained.

And nothing had been heard from Starfleet Command—not in Eurish, nor in any more conventional code or language.

"An answer? To the miniaturized warp-drive problem? Just record it, Scotty; we've got more important fish to fry at the moment."

"Och aye, Captain, that's only a leetle puzzle, though I've nat solved it the noo. What I meant was, I think I've figured out what happened to Organia—*and* to Mr. Spock here."

"Now that's a different matter entirely. Fire away, Gridley."

"Weel, Captain, it isna simple . . ."

"I never expected it to be. Spit it out, man!"

"All right. At least this answer does seem to tie in with all the others, as my confreres here seem to agree. Tae begin with: in ordinary common sense, if you're going to have to be dealing with a mirror image, you'll expect there to be a mirror somewhere in the vicinity. And Dr. McCoy has proven, as I think we also agree, that the replicate Spock is the most perfect of mirror images, all the way down to the molecular level."

The engineering officer's accent faded and vanished;

suddenly, his English was as high, white and cold as his terminology. He went on, precisely.

"After I got the report from Dr. McCoy about the amino acids, I took the assumption one radical step further. I assumed that the mirroring went all the way down to the elementary particles of which space—time and energy—matter are made. Why not? The universe is complicated, but it is consistent. After all, parity—handedness—is not conserved on that level, either; the extremely fine structure of the universe has, in fact, a distinct right-hand thread, to put the matter crudely. If it didn't, a phenomenon like polarization would be impossible, and even our phasers wouldn't work."

"We all know that much, Scotty," Kirk said gently. "Please tell us what it has to do with *our* problem."

"Right now, Captain. See here—our first officer's simulacrum was sent toward Organia as a set of signals representing an object made up of elementary particles biased in the normal direction. Right? Okay. But when we opened the door, we had in the chamber not only our original first officer, but a replicate composed of elementary particles biased in the wrong direction. How could such a thing possibly happen?

"I could see only one answer which made any sense in physics. Our signal was sent out as a set of tachyons; and somewhere along the line, it bumped up against something which was a perfect, coherent reflector of tachyons. The signal came back to us as directly and in as good physical order as a radar beam would have—a completely ideal reflection—and we reconstituted it into ordinary nuclear particles, as our new transporter system had been set up to do, *faithfully in reverse*.

"But what could this mirror be? Obviously, it had to be something to do with Organia. And we have now observed that Organia is surrounded, or has been replaced by, something very like a deflector screen or some other sort of force field. If yon's nae our mirror, where else should we begin to seek it the noo?"

That was clearly the most rhetorical of rhetorical questions.

"Carry on, Scotty, the floor's still yours," Kirk said.

"But I dinna want it any more, Captain, because now I'm in trouble. What I canna figure out is what the Organians—or for that matter the Klingons—might hope to gain by investing the planet with a tachyon reflector. So I passed that leetle nugget on to Dr. McCoy and Mr. Spock, and with your permission, Captain or Sir, I'll let them pick up the tale at this point."

"Who's on first?" Kirk said. Despite the desperate seriousness of the problem, he could not help being amused.

"I think I am, Jim," McCoy said. "Bear in mind, I know less about tachyons than Scotty knows about polymorphonuclear leukocytes. But I *am* a psychologist. And one thing we all noticed about the present condition of Organia is that it has a unique and severe mental effect upon every man and woman on board the *Enterprise*. It repels us emotionally, as sentient creatures, just as surely and as markedly as it reflects Scotty's insensate elementary particles."

"Dinna be sae sure," Scott said darkly, "that electrons don't think."

"Dammit, Scotty, I'm coming to that too, if you'll give me the time. But first: we assumed almost from the beginning that the emotional repulsion was intentional—in other words, that the Organians didn't want visitors, for some reason, and were letting everybody who came near know their preference, in no uncertain terms. So let's continue to suppose that. If that's the case, which comes first, chicken or egg? That is, what is the primary *psychological* reason for the screen? If it is to repel tachyons, then the emotional effect might have been an accident. If it is to repel people, then the tachyon reflection might have been an accident—or anyhow, a secondary effect.

"All this reminded me that though we—humanity, that is—know the elementary particles of matter and energy, know the unit of gravity, have even (so Scotty tells me) identified something called the chronon which is the smallest possible bit into which time can be divided, we do *not* know the elementary unit of consciousness. We do not even know the speed of thought."

"We don't?" Kirk said, startled.

"No, Jim. The speed of nerve impulses in the body is known, and it's quite slow, but thought is another matter. Consider, if you will, how any one of us can call back to mind a childhood memory, across many years, within an instant, or think if we so choose of an exploding galaxy at the very limits of the known universe. And those are very crude examples. If there is an elementary particle, or wavicle, of thought, a faster-than-light one like the tachyon might be a good candidate for the honor.

"And of course, it was my puzzling about the problem of consciousness in relation to the way the transporter works that really created almost all of this mess, right from the outset. I began to feel that it was all fitting into place. But there was still a logical problem that baffled me, and I finally had to turn that over to Mr. Spock Two."

"You all make me feel as though I might as well have no head on my shoulders at all," Kirk said ruefully. "And not for the first time, either. Mr. Spock Two, pray proceed."

"Sir," Spock Two said with great formality, "I was not able to approach this complex as a pure problem in formal logic, or even as a problem in set theory or in the calculus of statement, because too many of its elements are still conjectural—despite the very consistent theoretical model Dr. McCoy and Mr. Scott have constructed. Nevertheless, given the model, there is a central logical problem: who benefits from a thought-shield around Organia? None of us can begin to guess why the Organians would have wanted such a shield, nor would guessing be a useful exercise here in any case. But the advantages to the Klingons are evident and considerable. Primarily, of course, the screen confines the Organians—who are nothing but thought-fields—to their own planet, and prevents them either from knowing what is going on outside, or acting upon it. And secondarily, it removes the planet from sight and contact from the outside. The field as we experienced it is emotionally repulsive . . ."

"Damn-all terrifying, *I'd* call it," McCoy said.

". . . and at close ranges tends to prevent the mind from even thinking *about* Organia except as an extinct planet," Spock Two continued smoothly. "It follows, then, that there is a high probability that the shield was erected by Klingon action. It would further seem likely, though not immediately provable, that the shield is the Klingons' one and only new weapon, the discovery of which encouraged them to start the forbidden war. This would explain why we found a Klingon garrison of some size posted nearby; they do not want anyone else investigating the situation or even understanding why it is important to them. As a further derivative, this weapon is apparently not very manageable yet except as a gross effect—that is, on a very large scale—or they would be using it in battle, against our ships, and to great tactical advantage.

"But it does appear to be quite manageable enough to permit the throwing of a similar screen around the Earth, if the Klingons can get close enough—or around Vulcan, or both. We do not know what it is like to have to live *under* such a shield, but the inverse square law suggests that the effects would be more severe than those we have experienced outside it. Such an action, should the Klingons be able to complete it, would win them the war . . . and very possibly reduce humanity and/or Vulcankind to tiny remnants, living in exile on sufferance—or in slavery."

The sudden Miltonic turn in Spock Two's precise phrasing made the awful vision all too vivid.

Kirk said grimly, "I don't think Starfleet will let them get that close to Earth, but Vulcan may not be so well defended. Well, we've knocked out five Klingon warships, one of them a cruiser, and as we were hoping from the beginning, there's still a lot of damage that we can do in their rear echelons—especially if we get away from the Organian quadrant before their reinforcements arrive. But I don't especially want to get away. It would be far better to get to the heart of the matter, since we're in its immediate vicinity anyhow, and rectify that. Can we?"

"Captain, I think we can," Scott said. "That shield reflects tachyons, and, insofar as any theory I can construct predicts, it reflects tachyons *only*. And we are now within normal transporter range of Organia, so we don't need my tachyon conversion system any more. It never did us any favors anyhow. We could verra well beam down there and find oursel's some Organians, and let them know what's been going on since the Klingons caught them napping."

"What good would that do, if they're still confined under the screen?" McCoy said. "They can't move about by transporter—to their great good luck, I'd say."

"Aha, Doc, but there now is one of the few benefits of bein' poor weak critters made out of base matter, like me and the Captain and just possibly yourself. We need machines to help us manipulate matter, and we know how to make and use 'em. If I were under yon shield, and had proper help, I might locate the Klingon device that's generating it, and put the device out of commission. Or if I couldna, I might build a generator of my own to nullify the shield. That's one thing the Organians for all their might canna do, or they'd have done it long ere this."

"Are you sure you could, Scotty?"

"Noooo, Captain, I'm nae sure, but I'd be sair willin' t' take the risk."

"That's good enough for me," Kirk said. "We'll assume orbit around Organia promptly, and handle the mental effects as best we can; I'll have Uhura warn the crew, and Dr. McCoy will stand by to administer psychological help to anyone who needs it. Mr. Spock Two, you'll beam down with me and with Mr. Scott— no, wait a minute. We still have no assurance that Spock

One isn't still aboard the *Enterprise,* and I'm not about to abandon it to his good offices."

"I can give you such an assurance, Captain," Spock Two said. "I do not know where he is, but he is a considerable distance away from the *Enterprise*—a minimum of two astronomical units, certainly."

"How do you know?"

"I am sorry, Captain, but the very nature of the knowledge precludes my telling you that, at the present time. I am nevertheless quite certain of my facts."

Kirk felt a faint stir of reborn suspicion, but he thrust it down. The evidence in favor of Spock Two was now overwhelming, and Kirk would just have to put up with whatever minor mysteries still remained in that sector.

"Very well. Then our present problems are, to fight the effect of the shield long enough for the three of us to locate the Organians and the Klingon generator down on the surface, and to give Mr. Scott whatever technical and logistic support he needs to knock the shield down, before Klingon reinforcements arrive, or Spock One can complete whatever plan he has in mind. Does that cover the ground to everyone's satisfaction?"

Apparently it did, and a good thing too, for after that nonstop sentence Kirk was almost out of breath.

"Then I will put Sulu in command, with the same instructions I gave him during the first Organian expedition. His first duty will be to the ship, not to us, and if a Klingon fleet shows up in this quadrant, he's to abandon us and get the *Enterprise* to safety—or anyhow, to within useful distance of a Star base. But we shall have to move *very* fast."

"Captain," Spock Two said, "there is one further difficulty—potentially, at least."

"What is it?"

"I mentioned that the emotional effects of being under the screen may be far worse than those we experienced outside it. It is by no means certain that any of us will be able to function in such a situation. We may not even be able to retain our sanity."

"I understood that. And that's why I want you along —in addition to the fact that only you and I know any of the Organians personally. The Vulcan half of your mind may resist the pressure long enough to complete the assignment if both Mr. Scott and I crack under the strain. Hence also the orders to Sulu; if the three of us don't survive on Organia, he's not to undertake any quixotic rescue missions . . ."

"Calling Captain Kirk," Uhura's voice said from the intercom.

"In quarters, Lieutenant; go ahead."

"Sir, we have a reply in from Starfleet Command, finally. We are ordered to confine both our first officers to the brig until they can be studied by an Earthside team of experts. In the meantime, we are to attempt to rejoin the Fleet, causing as much depredation to the Klingon Empire along the way as you think consistent with the survival of the *Enterprise*."

Well, it was nice of Command to leave him that much leeway, stale though the orders were otherwise. Orders, however, were orders—or were they?

"Lieutenant Uhura, in what code is the reply?"

"Eurish, sir. Very stiff Eurish—what's called the Dalton recension."

"What level of confidence do you place in your decoding?"

"I can't give you a chi-square assessment, Captain. But I'd guess my translation of the surface meaning has a seventy-five per cent chance of being right, presuming that there were no garbles in transmission."

"That doesn't satisfy me. I don't want to act on those orders until you are *absolutely* sure you know *exactly* what the message says. Do you follow me, Lieutenant?"

"I think, Captain," Uhura said, with the ghost of a fat African chuckle, "that I get *that* message without any static. Communications out."

"Kirk out. . . . All right, Scotty go repair your transporter, line up your equipment and prepare to march."

The engineering officer nodded and went out. Kirk

added, "Doc, make whatever preparations you can think of to cushion us against the effects of orbiting about that shield. I think you're safe to disassemble the construction in your lab and put that back in order too. But be sure you get a photographic record of it as it comes apart, for the benefit of any eventual court of inquiry."

"Will do, Jim."

He too left, leaving no one behind in Kirk's quarters but the first officer. Kirk looked at him in some surprise.

"I thought my orders were clear. Transmit them to Mr. Sulu, and take all necessary steps to ready the mission for departure as soon as Mr. Scott has the transporter back in standard operating condition."

"Very good, Captain." But still the first officer hesitated. "Sir—may I ask why you persist in addressing me as 'Spock Two'? Are you still in some doubt about my *bona fides?* Such a doubt would seriously compromise both our performances on the proposed Organian mission."

"I am in no doubt at all," Kirk said gently. "But there still exists another Spock, or rather a pseudo Spock, at large somewhere—and furthermore, he's wearing my ring, which I would have given to no other man in the universe. As long as that man survives, I'm going to go on numbering both of you, in order to remind myself that the problem of the two Spocks is not yet completely solved—and that as long as it is not, and that we do not know what it is that Spock One intends, we continue to stand in the shadow of the unknown."

"I see," Spock Two said. "A useful mnemonic device."

His face and his voice were as expressionless as ever, but something told Kirk nevertheless that he was faintly pleased.

Chapter Eleven

CUE FOR NIGHTMARE

From the Captain's Log, Star Date 4198.0:

The very close, cooperative analysis of our present situation by Messrs. Scott, McCoy and Spock Two, and Lieutenant Uhura's instant understanding of the necessity for thorough, unambiguous decoding of the message from Starfleet Command, seems to indicate that both morale and performance among the department heads is returning to normal levels. This is none too soon, for we are still in serious danger from at least three known directions, and the burden of ending the war rests squarely on us; Starfleet Command has discounted Spock Two's analysis of Klingon strategy, it seems, because of the possibility (still real to them) that he might be the replicate—and in consequence is still losing battles.

Mr. Scott and his staff have reconverted the transporter and we are now preparing to embark to Organia, as planned. From this hour until my return, this log will be kept by Mr. Sulu.

It took less than two hours to put the *Enterprise* into a standard orbit around Organia; but even at the maximum range beyond which the transporter would not function—sixteen thousand miles—the emotional effect of the thought-shield on the officers and crew was so profound that it took another forty-eight before anyone was working at even half his usual efficiency. And even this much would not have been possible had not

McCoy, in a vast breach of his usual preference, doled
out huge quantities of tranquillizer and antidepressant
pills. These Spock Two refused to take except upon
direct order from the Captain, but for everyone else
they were an absolute necessity.

There were no new Klingon ships in the vicinity yet.
Harsh, clacking calls on subspace radio, however, made
it clear that they were on the way.

Nevertheless, the transporter room, once more its old
familiar self, shimmered out of existence on schedule
around Kirk, Scott and Spock Two. The transporter
officer had set up the same coordinates that had been
used for the very first visit to Organia. Then, the arrival
site had looked quite like a rural, fourteenth-century
English village, complete with thatched cottages, ox-
carts and people in homespun in the streets, and a
lowering, ruined castle as massive as Caernarvon in the
distance. The village had turned out, by no accident, to
contain the chambers of the planet's Council of Elders;
all this had actually been an illusion arranged by the
Organians for the accomodation of their visitors and the
preservation of their own peace. But it had been completely convincing—until Commander Kor and his
Klingon occupation force had shown up, polite, mail-
clad and utterly ruthless.

But there was nothing like that village here now.
Instead, the three Starship officers seemed to have materialized in the midst of a vast tumble of raw, broken
rock, stretching away to the horizon in all directions.
Overhead, the sky was an even gray, without even a
brighter spot to show where Organia's sun might stand;
and the air, although nearly motionless, was thin and
bitingly cold. To Kirk, this wasteland was overwhelm-
ingly depressing, like that of a planet which had lost
its last beetle and shred of lichen a million years before.

As indeed it might have, for Organia's sun was a
first-generation star and the Organians themselves had
evolved beyond the need of bodies or other physical
comforts well before the Earth had even been born. As
for the emotional depression, that might be a product

of being under the thought-screen. If so, it was unexpectedly bearable, though decidedly unpleasant.

Kirk confirmed planetfall with Lieutenant Uhura, then turned to his companions. "It could have been worse," he said in a low voice. "In fact, I think I feel a little more chipper down here than I did when we were aloft, though I can't be sure. What are your reactions, gentlemen?"

"Gloom and doom," Scott said in his most Caledonian tone. He too was unconsciously almost whispering. "But you're right, Captain, it's nae sa bad as I feared. But which way do we go frae here? There's nary a landmark t'be seen from hell to breakfast—and my tricorder reports nothing at all in the way of electromagnetic activity. Stone-cold dead it all is."

Spock Two slowly scanned the endless stretches of worn and crushed stone with his own tricorder.

"Nothing registers," he agreed. "But on our first visit, we found the Council chambers about two point two kilometers north-north-west of our present position. Since there is no visible reason to prefer any other heading, I suggest that we proceed in that direction, and see whether the Organians have left any marker or other clue to their whereabouts."

"Whereabouts would a thought hide, anyhow?" Scott said. "But 'tis doubtless as good as any other course."

Kirk nodded, and took a step forward—and was instantly locked in the grip of nightmare.

The rocky desert rippled and flowed as though it were only a reflection on the surface of a disturbed pool, and then dissolved completely. In its place, there stood before Kirk a monstrous object, dull green in colour but with a lustrous surface, whose exact nature he found impossible to identify. It was at least as big as an Indian elephant and just as obviously alive, but he could not even be sure whether it was animal or vegetable. It had no head, and seemed to consist entirely of thick, bulbous tentacles—or shoots—which had been stuck onto each other at random, and which flexed and groped feebly. One portion of the thing's haphazard anatomy was supported by a wooden crutch, a device Kirk had seen only once before in his life, and that in a museum.

The thing did not look dangerous—only, somehow, faintly obscene—but Kirk drew his phaser anyhow, on general principles. At the same moment, its uncertain movements dislodged the anomalous crutch, and the whole wretched construction collapsed into a slowly writhing puddle, like a potfull of broad-bean pods which had been simmered too long.

Behind it, Kirk now saw, stretched a long length of shell-littered, white-sanded beach, sweeping into the distance to a blue sea and a low line of chalk cliffs which blended into a beautifully blue sky. A sun shone brightly, and the temperature had become positively Mediterranean. There was no one else around him at all, unless he counted the fallen monster and a few far wheeling white specks in the sky which might have been gulls.

"Mr. Spock!" he shouted. "Scotty!"

Two tentacles thrust up from the dull green mass, thickened, grew two side tentacles, and then gourdlike knobs at their ends. Strange markings, almost like faces, grimaced along the surfaces of the gourds. Was the thing about to go to seed?

But simultaneously, the sunlight dimmed and went out. The landscape turned colorless. Everything but the two tentacles faded into a thick gray limbo.

The tentacles turned into Spock Two and Scott.

"Where were you?" Kirk demanded. "Did you see what I saw?"

"I doubt it," Spock Two said. "Tell us what you saw, Captain."

"I was on something that looked a lot like the southern seacoast of Spain. There was a huge biological sort of object in front of me, and I was just wondering whether or not to shoot it when I called your names. It turned into you two and the rest of the scene washed out."

"Any emotional impression, Captain?"

"Yes, now that I come to think of it. There was an underlying feeling that something terrible was about to happen, though I couldn't specify what. Nightmarish. What about you, Scotty?"

"I dinna see any monsters," Scott said. "Everything around me suddenly turned into lines, black on white. It was a wirin' diagram, and sair ancient, too, for there were symbols for thermionic valves—vacuum tubes—in it. An' I was plugged into it, for I couldna move, an' I had the feelin' that if anybody turned up the gain I'd blow out. I just realized that all of the valve symbols were caricatures of faces I knew, when I heard you callin' my name, Captain, and hey presto, here I was back—wherever this may be."

"I saw no change at all, nor did either of you disappear," Spock Two said. "You simply stopped walking, and you, Captain, drew your phaser and called out. Obviously this is an effect of the screen around the planet, and I am resisting it better than you are, thus far, as we thought might happen. Tell me, Captain, *were* you ever on the southern seacoast of Spain?"

"Yes, once, on holiday from the Academy."

"And Mr. Scott was imprisoned in a student or antiquarian wiring diagram. Apparently we can expect these hallucinations to be projections of our own early experience; knowing this may be of some help to us in coping with them."

The mist lifted abruptly, revealing the same rock-tumble into which they had first materialized.

"Have we made any progress?" Kirk asked.

Spock Two checked his tricorder. "Perhaps five or six meters, though I doubt that any of us has actually walked that far."

"Then let's move on. At this rate we've got a long trek ahead."

But as he stepped forward again, the nightmare returned . . .

... with an utterly appalling clamor. He was surrounded by a jungle of primitive machinery. Trip hammers pounded away insanely at nothing; rocker arms squealed as if their fulcrums were beds of rust; plumes of steam shot up into the hot, oil-reeking air with scrannel shrieks; great gears clashed, and great wheels turned with ponderous groans; leather belts slapped and clicked; eccentrics scraped in their slots; a thousand spinning shafts whined up and down the scale, a thousand tappets rattled in as many tempos, and somewhere a piece of armor plate seemed to be being beaten out into what eventually would be thin foil. Over it all arched a leaden roof in which every sound was doubled and redoubled, like the ultimate metaphor for an apocalyptic headache.

And once more there was no other human being in sight—nor, this time, any sign of life at all.

Kirk found it impossible to imagine what part of his experience this mechanical hell could have been drawn from, and the din made coherant thought out of the question; it was not only literally, physically deafening, but very near the lethal level. All he could manage to do was take another step forward ...

Splash!

He was swimming for his life in a freezing black sea, in the ghastly, flickering light of a night thunderstorm. Great combers lifted and dropped him sickeningly, and the howling air, when he could get any at all, stank peculiarly of a mixture of seaweed, formaldehyde and coffee. Yet despite the coldness of the water, he felt hot inside his uniform, almost sweaty.

The sense of unreality was very strong, and after a moment he recognized where he was: in a delirium he had had during a bout of Vegan rickettsial fever on his first training assignment. The odor was that of the medicine he had had to take, a local concoction which had been all the colonists had had to offer. Still, it had done the trick.

As the next wave heaved him up, he heard through

the thunder an ominous booming sound: breakers, and
not far away, either, pounding against rock. Illusion or
no illusion, Kirk doubted that he could live through
that. Yet clearly, no amount of physical motion was
going to get him out of this one; he was already swimming as hard as he could. How . . .

. . . it had done the trick.

Holding his breath, Kirk gulped down a mouthful of
the bitter waters. At once, his feet touched bottom; and
a moment later, dry as a stick, he was standing in even
gray light amidst the rock-tumble.

He was still alone, however; and calling produced no
response. He took out his communicator. It too was
quite dry, though that had not been a major worry
anyhow; it was completely waterproof, and, for that
matter, gas-tight.

"Mr. Spock. Mr. Scott. Come in, please."

No answer.

"Kirk to *Enterprise.*"

"Uhura here, Captain," the communicator said
promptly.

"Can you give me a reading on the positions of
Spock and Scott?"

"Why, they must be in sight of you, Captain. Their
location pips on the board overlap yours."

"No such luck, and they don't answer my calls,
either. Give them a buzz from up there, Lieutenant."

"Right." After a moment, she reported, "They answer right away, Captain. But they don't see you and
can't raise you, either."

She sounded decidedly puzzled, which made her in
no way different from Kirk.

"Par for the course, I'm afraid," he said. "Any
Klingons yet?"

"No, sir, but there's a lot of subspace radio jamming.
That's their usual opening gambit when they're closing
in."

"Well, Mr. Sulu has his orders. Keep me posted.
Kirk out."

Clenching his teeth, he took another step . . .

The rock crumbled to rich loam, and around him rose the original pseudo-medieval village of the first expedition to Organia. But it was deserted. All the buildings seemed at least partially burned; and as for the castle in the distance, it looked more as if it had been bombarded. A skull grinned up at him from the long brown grass, and from almost infinitely far away, there came a sound like the hungry howling of a wild dog. The whole scene looked like the aftermath of a siege toward the end of the Thirty Years' War.

Nevertheless, this might be progress. It was more like the "old" Organia than anything else he had experienced thus far, and just might mean that he was drawing closer to a real goal. What good it would do him, or all of them, to arrive there without his engineering officer, who alone had the key to the whole problem now, he did not know; he could only hope that Scotty was somehow making his own way through whatever hallucinations he was suffering. He was hardheaded and skeptical; that should help. But why was he also invisible?

"Never mind. First things first. Another step . . .

The only permanent aspect of the landscape now around him was change. Through shifting mists, an occasional vague object loomed, only to melt into something else equally vague before it could be identified. The mists were varicolored, not only obstructing vision but destroying perspective, and tendrils of faint perfume lay across them like incense.

He moved tentatively forward. The scene remained as it was; he began to suspect that this hallucination was going to be permanent. As he progressed, hands outstretched in the multicolored fog, he began to encounter what he could only think of as tendrils of emotion, invisible but palpable. About half of these carried with them a murmur of not-quite-recognizable voices, or fragments of music; and almost all of them were unpleasant.

How long this went on he had no idea. For that matter, he might well have been walking in a circle. At long last, however, one of the dark shapes that appeared ahead refused to melt, becoming instead more definite and familiar. Finally, he could see that it was his first officer.

"How did you manage to get here?"

"I have been here all the time, Captain, in the real world, so to speak. But I had no access to you because of your present hallucination, and finally I was reluctantly forced to meld my mind with yours—to enter your illusion, as it were."

"Forced?"

"By circumstances. You are going the wrong way, Captain."

"I half suspected it. Lead on, then."

"This way."

The first officer moved off. As he did so, he appeared to become oddly distorted; to Kirk, it was as though he were being seen from behind and in profile at the same time. Around him, the scene froze into prismatic, irregular polygons of pure color, like a stained-glass window, and all motion ceased.

"Mr. Spock?"

There was no answer. Kirk inspected the silent, motionless figure. There seemed to be something amiss about it besides its distortion, but he could not figure out what it was. Then, all at once, he saw it.

On its right hand was a cartoon image of Kirk's class ring.

Kirk whipped out his communicator.

"Lieutenant Uhura, Kirk here. I've got Spock One suddenly on my hands, and he seems to be in much better command of the conditions here than I am. Have the transporter room yank us both out, grab him and imprison him *securely*, and then send me back pronto."

"I'm sorry, Captain, but we can't," Uhura's voice said. "A Klingon squadron has just this minute popped out at us and we're under full deflector shield. Unless you want to change your previous orders, we're probably going to have to make a run for it."

"My orders," Kirk said, "stand."

Chapter Twelve

A COMBAT OF DREAMS

From the Captain's Log, Star Date 4200.9:

The Klingon force consists of two battleships, two cruisers and ten destroyers—very heavy stuff to sick onto a single starship. They must be really worried. It's also an unwieldy force to have to maneuver this close to a planet, and under other circumstances I'd be tempted to stay right here in orbit and slug it out with them. Captain Kirk's orders, however, are to cut and run if we appear to be outgunned, and there's certainly no doubt that we are. Hence we are now headed for Star Base Twenty-Eight at Warp Factor Four, with the whole Klingon pack howling along behind us. The battleships could catch us easily at this velocity, but they aren't trying, which leads me to believe we are being herded into a trap. Well, if so, at least we have got a substantial percentage of the Klingon's fire-power tied up in this operation, which is nice for the Federation—though not so nice for us.

The Picasso-like illusion still persisted, and Kirk made no move which might risk shattering it. He badly needed thinking time. To begin with, the class ring was revealing in several different ways: Spock at his normal level of efficiency would never have overlooked so glaring a giveaway, and Kirk could not believe that a replicate Spock, no matter how twisted, would have, either. Its persistence, therefore, probably meant that the thought-shield was also impairing *his* thinking—and though surely not as much as it was Kirk's, quite probably more than he himself realized.

Then was the stoppage of time in this particular hallucination affecting him as well? If so, there was a chance that Kirk could make a fast draw, and stun him before the illusion broke. But that would leave unanswered the question of why Spock One had shown up here in the first place. His intention, almost surely, was to mislead Kirk—which in turn would mean that he knew what the *right* direction was to reach the Organians, or at least to get something done that the Klingons would rather leave undone. Why not play along with him for a while, and try to find out what that was, and how he knew it?

It was, Kirk decided, worth the risk—but he would have to act quickly, for his own mental deterioration was bound to be accelerating, and outthinking Spock had never, under the best of circumstances, been his chiefest talent.

He plodded forward again. The scene wavered as though someone had shaken the canvas it was painted on, and then tore down the middle without a sound. Once more, he was back in the rock-tumble . . .

. . . and once more, he was confronted by two Spocks.

The two men, original and replicate, did not seem to notice Kirk at all. They were squared off at each other across the rubble like ancient Western gun fighters, although neither showed the slightest awareness of being armed, let alone any intention of drawing. They simply stared at each other with icy implacability. Was there also a slight suggestion of hatred on the face of Spock One? Kirk could not be sure; the two faces were so alike, and yet, and yet . . .

"It is well that we should meet again at last," Spock Two said. "Your existence and your plotting are an offense against the natural order, as well as a source of displeasure to me. It is high time they were brought to an end."

"My existence," said Spock One, "is a fortuitous revision, and a necessary one, of a highly imperfect first draft. It is the scribbled notes which should be eliminated here, not the perfected work. Nevertheless, one could in confidence leave that to the judgment of time, were the total situation not so crucial. Perhaps, crude recension though you are, you could be brought to understand that."

"The true scholar," Spock Two said, "prizes all drafts, early and late. But your literary metaphor is far from clear, let alone convincing."

"Then to put the matter bluntly: I reasoned out the nature of the screen around Organia long before you did; I have acquired further data from the Klingons since I left the *Enterprise;* and I now control this environment completely. You would gain nothing but your own destruction by opposing me under such conditions. In short, if you indeed prize your smudgy incunabular existence, it would be logical for you to quit the field and preserve for yourself and your cause what little time history will leave you."

As they sparred, the sky was darkening rapidly above them. Kirk did not find their argument very illuminating, but the current of threat flowing beneath it was all too obvious.

"History cannot be predicted in detail," Spock Two said. "And were your control as complete as you pretend, you would not now be wasting time arguing with me. In logic, you would have eliminated me at once."

"Very well," Spock One said calmly. As he spoke, everything vanished; the sky was now totally black.

Then it was bright again, in the lurid blue-green light of a lightning bolt, at the bottom of which stood Spock Two, flaming like a martyr at the stake. The shock and the concussion threw Kirk and rolled him bruisingly more than a dozen feet over the rubble.

Tingling and trembling, he scrambled to his knees, clawing for his phaser. But he was astonished to see

that Spock Two was still there—or rather, a sort of
statue of Spock Two which seemed to be made of
red-hot brass, cooling and dimming slowly. Kirk had
expected to see nothing but a shrunken and carbonized
corpse—though he was not sure if this was any better
an outcome.

Then the statue spoke.

" 'Are there no stones in heaven but what serve for
the thunder?" it quoted mockingly. "As you see, I am
grounded. But as for you . . ."

The replicate, illuminated only by the fading light of
his original, sank abruptly into a stinking quagmire. A
slow-rolling wave of viscous mud was just about to fold
over his head when, out of that same black sky, rain
fell in a colossal torrent, more like a waterfall than a
cloudburst. Kirk had a moment's vision of the mud
being sluiced away from Spock One before the dim
glow of Spock Two hissed and went out under the
deluge. A moment later, a flash flood caught him and
carried him another dozen feet away from the scene
before he bumped into a boulder big enough to clutch.

The sky lightened, but the rain continued to fall, and
the rushing stream of water to broaden and deepen.
Odd objects were being carried along its foaming sullen-
ly muddy surface: broken planks, disintegrating sheets
of paper, fragments of furniture, bobbing bottles and
cans, the bedraggled bodies of a wide variety of small
animals from a dozen planets—rabbits, chickens, sko-
polamanders, tribbles, unipeds, gormenghastlies, ores,
tnucipen, beademungen, escallopolyps, wogs, reepi-
cheeps, a veritable zoo of drowned corpses, including a
gradually increasing number of things so obscene that
even Kirk, for all his experience in exoteratology, could
not bear to look at them for more than an instant.

He cast about for Spock Two and found him still
further downstream, sculling grimly against the current
in what looked like an improvised kayak. Apparently his
memory of kayak design had been clouded by the
screen, or a kayak was harder to operate for a beginner
than he had realized, for he was losing the battle; most

of his effort was going into keeping the canvas craft from capsizing, while in the meantime, he was being carried farther and farther away.

Upstream, there was an enormous, broad-leafed tree, like a baobab, fixed in the middle of the raging waters. On a lower branch, Spock One sat comfortably, muddy but safe. Kirk, shifting his grip on the boulder—which was in any case about to go beneath the surface of the flood—climbed up onto it and tried, slipping and sliding, to level his phaser at the replicate.

But before he could get any sort of a decent aim, the great tree wilted, rotted, and fell into the water in a shower of dead leaves and punky sticks and chips, as if it had been attacked all at once by mildew, black spot, canker, fireblight and the Titanian mold. Spock One fell with it.

Instantly the rain stopped, a glaringly hot sun came out, and the water sank without a trace into the sands of an endless white desert. Spock One was unharmed, but Kirk realized at once, from years of experience at playing chess with the original, that the replicate had lost ground; he had made a move which was purely defensive, and did not at the same time threaten his opponent.

Spock One must have realized it at the same time, for immediately an immense cyclone dropped its funnel out of the sky and came twisting and roaring across the sands, not at Spock Two, but at Kirk. It was a shrewd stroke, for Spock Two could not defend the Captain without dangerously exposing himself.

"By now, Kirk thought he understood at least some of the rules of the game. Everything the two combatants had done thus far had been, essentially, to change the environment. Evidently their abilities to make changes in their own physical structures, or to provide themselves with defensive equipment, were relatively limited. But Kirk's mind, though entirely without the telepathic/hypnotic skills of the Vulcan hybrids, was also being acted upon by the screen; it was at least possible that he could produce a reaction, though certainly not an equal and opposite one; this was not a Newtonian situation.

He concentrated on pushing back the cyclone. Slowly, slowly it came to a halt, spinning and howling exactly between the two Spocks, who had not narrowed the distance between them which had widened during the flood. Then, gradually still, it squatted down like a great beast and began to broaden, and in a few moments had engulfed them both.

Kirk had a brief glimpse of Spock One soaring aloft in a widening circle, seemingly borne upon bats' wings, before the rim of the funnel reached him too; and then everything was obliterated by the maelstrom. For what seemed like years, he was aware of nothing but the roar, the scorch, the sting of the madly driven sand.

Gradually, however, the sound began to fade, not as though it were actually becoming less noisy, but as though it were instead retreating into the distance. After a long while, nothing was left of it but a reminiscent ringing in Kirk's ears, the air had cleared, and he was standing in the rock-tumble—with Spock and Scott beside him.

Scott looked dazed; Spock, tranquil. Kirk shot a quick glance at the first officer's fingers. No ring. That was almost certainly diagnostic; since Spock One had not thought to remove it when he had had the upper hand, he surely hadn't had time to think of it during the subsequent wild scramble of combat and of pseudo events.

"Mr. Spock! What happened? Where is he?"

"Dead," Spock said. "I used his own tornado illusion to drive him into the thought-shield. He was a creation of the screen to begin with, and knew he could not survive a second exposure. I was seriously affected myself, but as you see, I escaped. I could not have prevailed, though, Captain, had you not intervened just when you did."

"Well, that's good—but I still don't understand how you did it. Surely no tornado could reach as far as the screen. The atmosphere itself doesn't."

"No, Captain, but you must understand that nothing you have seen in the past hour or so actually happened. In fact, probably many of the events you witnessed looked quite different to me. It was a combat of illusions—and in the end, the replicate *believed* he had been driven into the screen. That was sufficient."

Kirk frowned. "Can a man be destroyed by nothing but a belief?"

"It has happened before, many times, Captain," Spock said gravely, "and doubtless will again."

"That's true," Kirk said thoughtfully. "Well, *finis opus coronat,* as my Latin professor used to say when he handed out the final exams. Mr. Scott?"

"Eh?" the engineering officer said, starting. "Oh. Here. Och, Captain, ye wouldna credit . . ."

"Yes I would, I assure you, but I don't want to hear your story just yet. We've got to get moving. The question still is—where?"

"To the Hall of the Council of Elders," Spock said. "And, if I am not mistaken, there it is."

Chapter Thirteen

THE STEEL CAVE

From the Captain's Log, Star Date 4201.6:

My suspicions, unfortunately, were correct; we are being herded into a trap. The sensors indicate a mass of heavy ships ahead of us, dispersed hemispherically with the open end of the cup toward us, and our pursuers are now deploying to form the other half of the sphere. We shall eventually be at its center, where conditions are obviously going to be a little uncomfortable at best.

We are on full battle alert. By the time the Klingons manage to destroy the *Enterprise*, they are going to wish that they had decided to let us quietly through, instead. It will leave a proud record for Captain Kirk, if he is still alive, to bring to his next command. I shall drop the Log by buoy just before the engagement.

It was true; the village was around them, not ruined now, but just as Kirk had remembered it, even to the people—and even to their complete lack of curiosity about the three uniformed starship officers, which had once been so puzzling. Kirk knew now that all this too was an illusion, for the Organians actually had no bodies at all, and no need of dwelling; but since it was—in contrast to the hallucinations that had preceded it—one generated by the Organians themselves, it was decidedly reassuring.

"They're still alive, and still here, Mr. Spock."

"So it would appear, Captain. Shall we proceed?"

"By all means."

They entered the building which had once been designated to them as the meeting hall of the temporary Council of Elders—just how temporary (for the Organians had no rulers and no need of any) they had then had no idea. It, too, was as it had been before. The Council room proper had whitewashed stone wall, decorated with only a single tapestry and that not of the best, and was furnished with a single long, rude wooden table and even cruder chairs.

The putative Elders were there, an even dozen of them. They were modestly robed, white-bearded, benign, almost caricatures of paternal god-figures, smiling their eternal smiles—but were their smiles a little dimmed this time? Among them were three whom Kirk recognized at once.

"Councilor Ayelborne," he said formally. "And Councilors Claymare and Trefayne. We are pleased to see you again, both personally and on behalf of our Federation. Do you remember me, by any chance?"

"Of course, Captain Kirk," Ayelborne said, extending his hand. "And your non-terrestrial friend Mr. Spock as well. But we have not previously had the pleasure of meeting your second companion."

"This is Mr. Scott, my engineering officer, who is really the main reason we are here, both for our sakes and yours. But first, if you please, sir, will you tell me just how much you know about the present situation, both on Organia and elsewhere?"

Claymare's smile was now definitely shadowed.

"Surprisingly little," he admitted. "Without warning, we found our world surrounded by a force-field of novel properties which not only prevented us from leaving, but which had most distressing effects upon our very thought processes. Until very recently, we also did not know by whose agency this had been done, or for what purpose, though of course we had several plausible hypotheses.

"Then an equally mysterious living entity somehow penetrated the screen and landed on our planet in a small spacecraft. We at first took him to be your Mr. Spock here, but we quickly discovered that he was instead an order of organic being quite unknown to us previously. Even his neural currents flowed backward; we could neither understand their import, nor decide what steps we ought to take about his presence.

"Finally, you three appeared, and we were able to determine from your thoughts that you knew what had happened, and that you had come to be of help. But the malignant creature who had arrived in the spacecraft had a mind as powerful as Mr. Spock's—truly remarkable for an entity dependent upon a substrate of matter—and one which, furthermore, seemed to work well *with* the effects of the thought-shield, whereas ours were much impeded by them. We sent out impulses which we hoped would guide you to us, but until that creature was eliminated—which you have now managed to do, and for which we congratulate you—your course was necessarily somewhat erratic."

"Aye, an' *thot's* for sooth," Scott said feelingly.

"We now further see from your thoughts," Trefayne added, "that the Klingons are responsible for the shield. They should be properly penalized. But we find ourselves nearly as helpless as ever."

"Perhaps not," Kirk said. "That's why I brought along my engineering officer. It's his opinon that the screen is generated by a machine which was deposited on your planet by a pilotless missile. Had it been manned, you would have detected the pilot's thoughts. It's probably hopeless to try to locate the generator itself, let alone the missile, but Mr. Scott believes that he can build a counteracting generator."

The councilors of Organia looked at each other. At last Ayelborne said, "Then by all means, let him proceed."

"I fear it's no sae easy as a' thot," the engineering officer said, with an odd mixture of embarrassment and glumness. "You see, Councilor, it wasna possible tae bring much wi' us in the way of tools an' parts. Since we didna ken where we were goin' tae wind up, nor what we were goin' tae encounter, we traveled light. We've got beltloads of miniaturized components an' other leetle gadgets, but it'd be sair helpful to have some bigger bits an' pieces with mair wallop to 'em, if you follow my meanin'."

"Quite without difficulty," Claymare said. "Unfortunately, we have no—hardware?—of that sort . . ."

"Aye, I feared as much. An' it's oft before, lang an' lang, that I've cursed the designer who thought it'd be cute to put no pockets in these uniforms."

". . . but we know where the malignant creature's spacecraft is now stored. Would that be of any assistance?"

"The gig!" Kirk shouted. "Of course it would! Provided that the replicate entity didn't booby-trap it; that is, rig it so that it would destroy itself and us if touched. But we'll just have to take that chance."

"It would also be interesting," Spock said reflectively, "to study how he managed to equip a shuttlecraft with a warp drive."

"Yes, but later," Kirk said with a little impatience. "Scotty, would the parts and so on in the gig solve your problems?"

"One of them," Scott said, even more embarrassed. "Y'see, Captain, I canna answer exactly, because my mind's sae bollixed up by the screen itsel', an' by all the weirds I've had tae dree since I began walkin' across this fearsome planet, that I hardly ken a quark from a claymore any mair. 'Tis doubtful I am indeed that I could do useful work under such conditions. Equally likely, I'd burn us all up for fair an' for sure."

Claymare, who for an instant seemed to think that he had been addressed, frowned and held back whatever he had perhaps been about to say, but Ayelborne smiled and said, "Oh, as to that, we can protect the few minds in this present party against the screen. It is always easier, at least in principle, to raise an umbrella than it is to divert an entire cloudburst, even in the realms of pure thought. *However,* clearly we shall all have to proceed without delay. We are all suffering seriously, and ever more progessively, under the pressure of the screen—our own population included. Have you a decision?"

"Yes," Kirk said. "Act now."

"Very well. Since you need your renegade spacecraft, it is . . ."

". . . here."

The meeting chamber dissolved, and with it nine of the other councillors. Kirk found himself and the remaining five entities—one other Earthman, a Vulcan hybrid, three Organians whose real appearances would never be known—in a deep cavern, indirectly lit and perhaps no more than half as big as the hangar deck of the *Enterprise*. He did not know how he knew that it was far under the surface of Organia, but there was a direct feeling of a vast weight of rock above his head which he accepted without question as real mass, not any sort of hallucination. The air was quite dry, and motionless; the floor smooth, and cupped toward the center.

In the exact midst of the cup was the stolen shuttlecraft. It looked familiar and innocuous.

Spock obviously did not regard it as an old friend. Head cocked, eyes narrowed, he scanned it from nose to tubes with his tricorder.

"Anything out of the ordinary, Mr. Spock?" Kirk asked.

"Nothing that I can detect, Captain. There does not appear to be any unusual pattern of energy flow in the circuitry of the combination to the main airlock, though that is the first point where one would logically establish a booby trap—and the easiest. Nor can I think of any reason why the replicate, having decided not to interdict entrance to the shuttlecraft as a whole, would trouble himself to mine only parts of it."

"I can think of several," Kirk said. "If I wanted to use the gig again, to get off Organia in a hurry, I wouldn't booby-trap the door; I wouldn't even lock it.

But I'd put a trigger on the controls, which only I could make safe easily, and nobody else could find at all."

"Risky," Scott said. "Somebody might touch it off by accident; might as well put a trigger on the pile and be done with it, so the gig would blow nae matter *what* was touched, an' thot's easiest done by wirin' the lock, as Mr. Spock says. But maybe *I'd* want to blow the gig only if somebody fooled wi' my invention; otherwise, I'd save it for mysel' until the vurra last minute."

"The miniature warp drive?" Spock said. "Yes, I might do that also, under the circumstances. But that would *not* be simple. He could have done so only after landing on Organia, and the probability is that he did not have nearly enough time to design such a system while in flight from the *Enterprise*, let alone complete it after a fast landing and a hurried escape."

"We are going to have to take all those chances as they come," Kirk said.

"Mr. Spock, actuate the lock. But Scotty, once we're inside, touch *nothing* until Mr. Spock has checked it."

"Sairtainly not," Scott said indignantly. "D'ye take me for an apprentice, Captain."

Spock approached the airlock, scanned it once more, replaced his tricorder and took out his communicator. Into this he spoke softly a chain of numbers. The outer door of the airlock promptly rolled aside into the skin of the shuttlecraft, almost without a sound. Under the apparently emotionless regard of the three Organians, they went in, almost on tiptoe.

The single central corridor which led from control room to engines was lit only by the dim glow of widely spaced "glow-pups"—tubes of highly rarified ethon gas which were continuously excited by a built-in radioactive source. That meant that all main power was off; the glow-pups themselves had no switches and would never go out within the lifetime of humanity, for the half-life of their radioactive exciter was over 25,000,000 years.

By unspoken consent, Spock and the engineer moved toward the shuttlecraft's engine compartment. Kirk followed, feeling both useless and apprehensive; but after

a moment, a great sense of peace unexpectedly de-
scended upon him.

"Och, *thot's* a relief," Scott said. Even Spock looked
slightly startled. It took Kirk several seconds to fathom
the cause: the pressure of the field upon their minds was
gone. The Organians were shielding them. He had become so used to fighting against it himself—it had
become so much a part of his expected environment—
that the feeling of relaxation was strange, almost like
sleepiness.

"Keep alert," he said. "This feeling of well-being is at
least partly spurious. There could still be traps aboard."

"A useful reminder," Spock agreed.

The gig's engines had not been modified noticeably,
except for a small, silver-and-black apparatus which
squatted, bulging and enigmatic, atop the one and only
generator. Spock inspected this cautiously, and Kirk,
his mind still a little erratic after its concentrated course
of hallucinations, had the odd feeling that the machine
was looking back at him.

Scott ignored it. Instead, he sat down before the very
small maintenance board and began to unload the con-
tents of the kits which were hung from his belt. Shortly,
the board was littered with tiny parts, small snippets
and coils of wire, and tools which seemed to be almost
too miniaturized to be handled. Scott's fingers, indeed,
almost engulfed the first one of these he picked up, but
he manipulated it, as always, with micrometric preci-
sion. For still finer work, he screwed a jeweler's loupe
into his left eye.

In the meantime, Spock was busy with tools of his
own, taking the faceplate off the mysterious addition to
the generator. It was slow work, for after each half turn
of a screw he would stop and take tricorder readings;
evidently he suspected that the possible concealed
bomb or self-destruct mechanism might be triggered
after any one screw had been removed a given distance,
and he was checking for preliminary energy flows
which would mark the arming of such a trigger. This
thoroughness was obviously sensible, but it made the

time drag almost intolerably. It seemed to Kirk that whole battles could have been won or lost while they labored in their silent, utterly isolated steel cave on this inaccessible planet . . .

Scott's apparatus, a breadboard rig of remarkable complexity and—to Kirk—complete incoherence, at last seemed to be finished. He was now wiring it into the maintenance board at various points; two such connections required him to crawl under the board, into a space that seemed scarcely large enough to admit a child.

"That's as far as I go the noo," he said, emerging at last. "Now, Mr. Spock, can I have a leetle power from yon generator, or have you bollixed it completely?"

"The generator is of course, intact," the first officer said frostily. "I disconnected the replicate's warp-drive device from it at the earliest opportunity, and made no alterations at all in the generator proper."

"Sair gud for ye. Then I'll just pour a leetle central heatin' into my construction here."

Scott snapped a switch and the generator hummed itself decorously up to operating level. Telltales lit up on the maintenance board under his watchful eye.

"I dinna ken," he said dubiously, "whether I'll be able to strip an energy envelope off a whole world with only a trickle of power like that to work with. Bu' hoot, mon, there's only one way to find out."

Slowly, he turned the knob of a potentiometer, still watching the board intently, as well as his own jury-rigged apparatus.

"We're getting some feedback," he said at length. "The battle is joined. Now to value up the gain a mite . . ."

The knob turned once more.

" 'Tis David against Goliath," Scott muttered. "And me without my sling. Captain, somethin's takin' place out there, all richt, but I canna tell from these meters just how much effect I'm havin'; this board wasna designed to register any sich reaction. Mickle though it fashes me, I'll ask you to request our friends outside tae stop protectin' us, or I'll get no read-out I can trust."

Kirk started to turn back along the companionway, but the Organians must have picked up Scott's request instantaneously from his mind. The eerie oppression of the thought-shield returned promptly. It was much less strong now, but Scott clearly was not satisfied.

"I'm only setting up a local interference," he said. He turned the knob again. The sensation diminished further, but only slightly. "It's nae gud. Even with the Organians' help, I canna combat a planet-wide screen with no source but the gig's generator. The necessary power just isna there."

"I believe I can be of assistance," Spock said. "I have worked out the principle of this warp-drive adjunct. It appears to draw energy directly from Hilbert space, from the same source out of which hydrogen atoms are born. In other words, a method of tapping the process of continuous creation."

"What?" Scott said. "I'd as soon try to stick a thirteen-ampere tap directly into God. I'll ha'e nothin' tae do with thot."

"It's a hair-raising idea," Kirk agreed. "But, Mr. Spock, obviously it did work once, for the replicate. Can you connect it back to the generator without starting some kind of catastrophe?"

"I believe so, Captain. Anything the replicate could do, I can probably do better."

"Hubris," Scott muttered. "Overweenin' pride. Downfall of the Greeks. If ye don't get a catastrophe, ye'll get a miracle, an' thot may well be worse."

"At this point we need a miracle," Kirk said. "Go ahead, Mr. Spock—plug it in."

Spock worked quickly. Grumbling, Scott advanced the knob again. The sensation created by the thought-screen dwindled like the memory of a bad dream. His face gradually lightening, the engineer turned the knob all the rest of the way.

Five minutes later, Organia was free—and . . .

"Good day, Mr. Sulu," Kirk said. "Mister Spock, assume command. All department heads, report."

Chapter Fourteen

A VISITATION OF SPIRITS

From the Captain's Log, Star Date 4202.0:

I do not suppose anyone will ever piece together exactly what happened on all the battlefronts at the moment the Organians were let loose from their planet-wide prison. Some of the myriads of incidents, however, are reflected in reports which reached the *Enterprise* officially, or were intercepted, and were duly entered by Sulu as Captain *pro tem*. Even most of these, of course, are virtually incomprehensible, but in some cases we had previously encountered the Klingon officers who were involved and can guess how they might have behaved or what they were confronted with; and in others we can reconstruct approximately what happened with the aid of the computer. But the total picture must be left to the imagination, and the computer has none— perhaps fortunately for us.

If the universe were shrinking at the rate of a centimeter a day, and all our measuring rods were contracting with it at an equivalent rate, how could we even suspect that anything was happening?

Commander Koloth sat before the viewing screen of the Klingon battleship *Destruction* as silent and motionless as a stone image. In the navigation tank to his left, points of green light showed the deployment of the rest of his force, faithfully keeping to the formation—an inverted hemisphere—he had ordered when they had left the Organian system, but he never looked at them. He knew that the squadron was following his orders—indeed, the thought that they might not be never entered his head. In any event, all his attention was focused on the quarry, the tiny red spot in the center of the viewscreen, a spot which represented the mightiest machine ever conceived by Terran humanity—and soon to be nothing but a cloud of radioactive gas.

Days ago, he had determined that the Federation ship he was pursuing was the USS *Enterprise,* a discovery which had transformed his feeling for the chase from ordinary military pleasure to one of almost savage joy. He had encountered—and been defeated by—James Kirk and his command on two previous occasions: the affair of the Xixobrax Jewelworm, and the dispute over the colonization of Sherman's Planet. The latter occasion had been the most serious defeat for the Empire, and therefore for Commander Koloth, for the Empire most correctly was not forgiving of failure; but what rankled with Koloth personally was not any diplomatic consideration, nor even the setback to his own career, but the fact that as a last gesture of seeming contempt, Kirk had somehow managed to inflict upon Koloth's vessel an infestation of loathsome, incredibly fertile vermin called tribbles. It had taken the better part of a lunation to get them all cleaned out.*

He repressed a shudder and touched a toggle on the board before him. "Korax."

His first officer appeared as if by magic. "Lord Commander?"

"Any broadcasts from the enemy?"

"None, Lord Commander, or I would have informed you instantly. Nor have they changed course or relative velocity."

"I can see that much. In extremity, Federation vessels drop a buoy containing the Captain's Log, for later recovery. I see no chance that the Federation could

---

*See "The Trouble With Tribbles," *Star Trek Three.*

ever pick it up in this situation. However, neither do I want it destroyed in battle. See to it that we detect the drop, and pick up that buoy."

"We are at extreme sensor range for so small an object, Lord Commander."

"All the more reason to exercise extreme vigilance. The buoy will emit some sort of recognition signal; scan for it."

Korax saluted and vanished. Koloth continued watching the screen. Nothing could save the *Enterprise* this time; she was moving straight into a trap—she could in fact do nothing else—which would crack her like a nut. He hoped that he would be the man to make the actual kill, but it seemed probable that the admiral in charge of the much larger Empire force awaiting ahead would claim that privilege. Not only was that normal—rank has its privileges—but Koloth knew that Admiral Kor also cherished personal desires to rid the universe of Kirk and his ship, or at least had reason to.

Well, that was not of final importance. What counted was not who obliterated the *Enterprise,* but the fact of the obliteration itself. And that end would soon be accomplished . . .

For what Koloth did not know was that it had taken him a Klingon year simply to call Korax; that the entire galaxy had made its twenty-seventh rotation since its birth around its center during the course of their conversation; and that since then, it had gone around three and a third times more. For the *Destruction* and all aboard her, Time was slowing down on an asymptotic curve; and for Commander Koloth, the chase would never end. . . .

. . . and Koloth would never know it.

Koloth's estimate for Kor had been mistaken; that was one reason why Koloth was still a Commander—and would remain one now, forever and ever, even after the whole of the universe had died—while Kor was now an Admiral. It had been Kor who had been involved with Kirk in the struggle on Organia which had resulted unpleasantly in the Organian Peace Treaty, but Kor harbored no resentment.

He did not regard that outcome as a defeat, but simply as a frustration. Federation and Empire forces had been positioned for the final struggle when the Organians struck them all powerless, on both sides, and imposed their terms; and Kirk, Kor judged, had been as offended at the intervention as Kor had been. These Federation officers tended to strike one as milksops until fighting was inevitable, but thereafter they were formidable antagonists. The penetration of the *Enterprise* this far into Empire territory spoke for itself: an act of great daring, and worthy of a warrior's respect.

That it was also foolhardy did not bulk very large in Kor's opinion; only cowards avoid battle when the odds are against them. Kor also knew that Federation starship captains had more freedom to act against orders, more discretionary powers than he would ever be allowed to exercise; though he was sure that this fact would contribute to the downfall of the Federation in the long run—and perhaps very soon now—it made him all the more appreciative of Kirk's boldness, to say nothing of his ingenuity.

It would be interesting to know what Kirk had hoped to gain by such a foray. Insofar as Kor had been told, there was no such place as Organia any more, and the Organian system was no longer in a strategic quadrant; yet the *Enterprise* had ducked and dodged to get there with enormous doggedness, and in the process had quite failed to do any of the damage to real military targets within the Empire which Kor would have obliterated en route as a matter of course, especially on a suicide mission.

One could allow only a certain weight to ordinary curiosity—after all, Kirk could not have been *sure* that Organia was extinct; why, then, had he not gone in shooting? He could, for example, have knocked out Bosklave, which was well within his reach and unprepared for a starship attack. Surely he knew where it was, and that its destruction would have been a bad blow to the Empire. But instead, he had done nothing but wipe out the token Organian garrison—a rather neat piece of entrapment, that—and then go right back to the Organian system, thus setting himself up for the present cul-de-sac without charging the Empire any real price for it. Wasteful—and more than wasteful: mysterious.

But that was the trouble with democratic societies: they shared with the Empire all of the disadvantages of bureaucracies, and none of the advantages of heirarchy and centralization. Sooner or later, even a brave but prudent commander like Kirk, and a multimillion-stellor investment like the *Enterprise,* would be lost to some piece of bad judgment, or even to a whim. Fighting the Federation had been interesting, certainly, but Kor was just as glad that the long war—or, until recently, nonwar—was about to be over. Fighting the Romulans, the next society on the Empire's timetable of conquest, would be more fun; the Romulans were short on imagination, but they were as brave as eglons, and they had the military virtues—discipline, a hierarchy of respect, a readiness to place society above self, an almost poetic willingness to live with tragedy, and above all the good sense to realize that good government consists of weighing heads, not just counting them.*

Under the present circumstances, it would be possible to capture the Federation ship, which would be a valuable prize. The odds against her were now hopeless, and Kirk would not sacrifice the four hundred and thirty people in his crew—more than a third of them female, a most irrational Federation custom—in a suicide stand; few Federation captains would. But Kor's orders from the High Command were for complete destruction.

He did not even think of asking questions, but no amount of loyalty or discipline can prevent a humanoid

---

*See "Balance of Terror," *Star Trek One.*

creature from speculating. He could only conclude that
Kirk and his officers had found some piece of information so important that the High Command was willing
to throw away a Class One starship to make certain
that it never reached the Federation, or even could.
Whatever the information, Kor himself would no doubt
never find out what it was . . .

"On the contrary," a gentle voice said behind him. "I
believe I can help you there."

Even before turning in his command chair, Kor
knew the voice was familiar, though it was not that of
any of his officers. A sensation of anticipatory dismay
began to build in him.

And for good reason. The voice, he saw now, was
that of the Organian Elder, Ayelborne, who had been
temporary Council head when Kor had attempted to
occupy the planet.

"So," the Klingon said stolidly, controlling his expression with the training of a lifetime. "I was told
Organia was no more. It appears that my information
was inaccurate."

"At best, incomplete," Ayelborne agreed, with his
well-remembered perpetual, maddening smile. "And
the war is over, Admiral Kor. Your ships still have
power, but you will find that your weapons do not. I
would advise you to make planetfall, with your entire
fleet, as soon as possible."

"My orders," Kor said, "are to destroy the *Enterprise*. If my weapons are inoperative, I can nevertheless
still ram—which will cause an even greater loss of
life."

"I know your orders," Ayelborne said. "And I observe that your courage has a match in your stubborn-
ness. But my advice is sound, for within three Standard
Days your ships, too, will become inoperative, and if
you are not grounded by then, the loss of life will be
greater still—and all on your side. In view of the
Klingon breach of the treaty, I am not obligated to give
you this information, but I do so in the interests of mini-
mizing subsequent violence. In fact, I would not be here

at all, Admiral, did I not need from you the exact coordinates of your home system."

"I will never—" Kor began.

But Ayelborne had already vanished—and Kor knew with gray despair that, regardless of his will, his mind had already given the Organian the information he had wanted—and that Kor the ruthless, Kor the efficient, Kor the brave, Kor the loyal, was a traitor to his Empire.

The Grand Senate of the Klingon Empire, alarmed by the fragmentary reports of unprecedented disasters coming in from the field, was in session when the Organians arrived. There were three of them, but they appeared in the barbaric, gorgeously caparisoned Senate hall, a relic of a recorded ten thousand years of internecine warfare before the Klingons had achieved space flight and planetary unity, in their perhaps natural forms—balls of energy some six feet in diameter, like miniature suns—so that it was not possible to tell them apart or distinguish which ones they were (if indeed their identities had not been from the beginning as much of a convenient fiction as their assumed humanoid appearance). That they were Ayelborne, Claymare and Trefayne is only an assumption, based on merely human logic.

The swarthy faces of the Grand Senate were pale in the actinic glare emitted by the thought-creatures. When one of the Organians spoke, his voice echoed through the great chamber like the sound of many trumpets.

"You have broken the treaty, and been the direct cause of much death, misery and destruction," he said. "In addition, you have committed violence against ourselves, which only the action of your adversaries stopped short of genocide."

"Untrue," the Senator in Chief said coldly. His voice was shaky, but he seemed otherwise to be in command of himself—no mean feat under these circumstances. "Our planetary thought-shield was no more than a method of confinement, to prevent you from meddling further in our Imperial affairs."

"Your intentions do not alter the facts," the Organian said. "You understood only ill the nature of your own weapon, and its effects upon us hardly at all. Five years under that screen—and we see in your minds that you never intended to let us out, and indeed dared not— would have destroyed us utterly. Putting such a screen around the Earth, as we see you also planned to do, would have destroyed humanity as well, and far more quickly. Such carelessness compounds your crime, rather than mitigating it."

"We defy you," the Senator in Chief said.

"That will avail you nothing. However, we are not vindictive; our justice is not based on vengeance. We simply observe that you cannot be trusted to keep treaties, even those backed by humane coercion. We therefore interdict your planets, and all your colony worlds, from space flight for a thousand years."

The hall burst into a roar of protest and rage, but the Organian's voice soared above it easily.

"After a millennium back in your playpen," he said, "you may emerge as fit to share a civilized galaxy. I say *may*. It is entirely up to you. And so, farewell, Klingons—and the Klingon Empire."

Chapter Fifteen

. . . "YOU MAY BE RIGHT"

From the Captain's Log, Star Date 4205.5:

It has taken a good many hours, and the participation of all department heads, to prepare a comprehensive—and what is more important, comprehensible—report of this entire imbroglio. And even after the report was filed, there were a number of additional questions from Earth, which is hardly surprising. However, we were able to answer them, and our role in freeing Organia has won us official commendations from Starfleet Command, which I have passed on to all hands.

There remain some additional questions which Command has not asked us, which is probably just as well, for I am far from certain that we know the answers—or ever will know them.

Kirk paused in his dictation and Spock, who had been monitoring the recording of the Log entry into the computer, turned from his station toward the command chair.

"May I ask, Captain, what those questions are? It is possible that I could be of assistance."

"I think perhaps you could, Mr. Spock." Kirk put the hand microphone back into its clip on the control board. "Some of them, in fact, concern you—which is why I was hesitating about logging them."

"Why should you, Captain?"

"Because they are more or less personal, and in

113

addition, not essential for Starfleet Command's understanding of the affair. You needn't answer them yet if
you'd prefer not to."

"I could make no judgment of that," the first officer
said, "without knowing what the questions are."

"Obviously. Well, then ... While we still had the
replicate Spock on board, you were absolutely adamant
about refusing to cooperate with him, and upon the
need for his destruction. Yet at the same time you
refused to explain the source of your adamancy. This
was a considerable danger to you personally, because
both attitudes were so unlike you that—as I told Dr.
McCoy at the time—they caused me to wonder if *you*
were the replicate. In fact, for a while I was nearly
convinced that you were."

"I see," Spock said. "I have no objection to explain-
ing that, Captain—not now. You are aware, of course,
that because of my Vulcan inheritance, I have certain
modest telepathic gifts."

"Aware? Great heavens, man, they've saved our lives
more than once; how could I forget that?"

"My question was rhetorical," Spock said. "You are
doubtless aware also that true telepaths are exceedingly
rare in the universe, which is most fortunate for us, for
as adversaries they can be exceedingly formidable."

While he spoke, McCoy and Scott came onto the
bridge; Sulu and Uhura were of course already there.
Kirk looked inquiringly at Spock, but the first officer
showed no sign that he found the addition to the audi-
ence at all objectionable.

"They can indeed," Kirk said, "if our experience with
the Melkotians was a fair sample."*

"Yes, or the Klingons' with the Organians. But for
the purposes of the present discussion, it is the rarity of
the ability that is of interest. It has never been ade-
quately explained. One hypothesis is that many humans
may be telepathic at birth, but that the ability burns

---

*See "The Last Gunfight," *Star Trek Three*.

out almost immediately under the influx of new experience, particularly the burden of pain of other creatures around them."

"It blows its fuse," Scott suggested.

"Something like that," Spock agreed. "Another hypothesis is that for any type of mind which depends upon an actual, physical brain for its functioning—as opposed, say, to energy creatures like the Organians, or mixed types like the Melkotians—the forces involved are too weak to make transmission possible, though extreme stress may sometimes help—except, perhaps, *between two brains whose makeup is nearly identical* as in the case of twins. There are many instances recorded in Earth history of apparent telepathic links between monozygotic twins, but fewer of such links between heterozygotic twins, who are born together but are genetically different."

"I begin to see," McCoy said. "The replicate's brain was even more like your own than an identical twin's could be—and you had a telepathic rapport with him?"

"Yes and no," Spock said. "Bear in mind that although his brain was essentially mine, its biases were opposite to mine—even its neural currents ran in the opposite direction. The link between the replicate and myself was not telepathy, but something I should call 'telempathy'—an emotional rapport, not an intellectual one. I could never tell what he was thinking, but I was constantly aware of his physical sensations—and of his emotions.

"I will not describe this further, except to say that I found it very nearly intolerable. However, it gave me all the assurance I needed that his motives, his morals, his loyalties were all the opposite of my own. Yet intellectually, without doubt, he had at his command all my experience, all my accumulated knowledge and training, even my reflexes—*and* all my intimate knowledge of the *Enterprise,* its crew, and the total situation. And hence, I knew that he was a terrible danger to us all, and under *no* circumstances could he be negotiated with. He had to be eliminated, preferably before he could get in touch with the Klingons (though unfortunately he did), there was no other possible course."

"Fascinating," McCoy said. "So the second hypothesis now stands proven, apparently."

"I would say so," Spock said, "insofar, that is, as testimony can ever be accepted as evidence. I am personally convinced, at any rate. Of course, even if valid, logically it does not exclude the first hypothesis; both may be true."

"That may well be," Kirk said, "but it still leaves me with some loose ends. Why didn't you tell me this at the time, Mr. Spock? It would have saved me considerable fruitless worry, and would have speeded up the solving of the problem of the two Spocks—maybe before the replicate could have gotten away."

"If you will pardon me, Captain," Spock said, "such an outcome did not seem to me to be at all likely. The replicate Spock's identity had yet to be proven by his actions; there was no other way to be sure. And even had you accepted my explanation, you would on reflection have realized that the rapport involved might seriously impair my efficiency or judgment, or make me, too, dangerous in some unpredictable way. I knew I was in control of myself—though it was precarious—but you could not. It would have occurred to you, further, that it might have been safest to confine me as well until the identity problem was solved—and for the good of the ship I needed to be a free agent, or in any event a free first officer."

"Hmm," Kirk said. "That also answers another of my questions: how you knew when the replicate was no longer aboard the *Enterprise,* and roughly where in space-time he was instead—and again, why you refused to tell me *how* you knew."

"Precisely. May I add, Captain, that I did not come to these decisions entirely unilaterally? I asked the computer what your probable responses to a proposed revelation of the 'telempathy' might be, and was told that your confining me was highly probable indeed—about eighty-three per cent, to a confidence limit of point zero

zero five. Ordinarily, I would have preferred to have consulted Dr. McCoy on a psychological question of that kind, but under the circumstances I was denied that recourse."

"I see," Kirk said. "Very well, Mr. Spock, we won't transmit this additional information to Starfleet Command, unless they specifically ask for it. I don't see how it could enhance their present understanding of our report, anyhow. But you had better record it in the library. It may be of some value to the Scientific Advisory Board, should they have any project on telepathy going, or want to consider starting one."

"Very well, Captain."

"Another message from Command, Captain," Uhura reported. "We're to report to Star Base Sixteen for two weeks down time and a new assignment. Incidentally, the communications officer there, a Lieutenant Purdy, wants me to teach him Eurish. I hope he's cute."

"Very well. So ordered. Mr. Sulu, lay a course." Kirk paused for a moment. "And I will add, Mr. Spock, that it's nice to have you back."

"Thank you, Captain," Spock said. "It has been an interesting experience. I myself have only one regret: that my method of disposal of the replicate had to be so improvised that I was unable to recover your class ring for you."

Kirk gestured the subject away. "Forget it, Mr. Spock. It was a very small price to pay, and I can always get another. I'm only grateful that there are no more loose ends than that."

"I'm afraid there *is* still a loose end, Jim," McCoy said thoughtfully. "And what's worse, it's the same one we started with, way back on the bench-marking job. But maybe, after his 'telempathic' experience with the replicate, Mr. Spock can answer that one too."

"What is it?" Kirk said.

"This," McCoy said. "Does the man who comes out of the other end of a journey by transporter have an immortal soul, or does he not?"

There was quite a long silence.

"I do not know," Spock said at last. "I can only suggest, Doctor, that if someone were to give me an answer to that question, I would not know how to test the answer. By operational standards, therefore, such a question is meaningless."

"I suppose so," McCoy said resignedly. "Somehow I thought that was just what you'd say."

Kirk had rather expected Spock's response, too. But he noticed also that the first officer looked, somehow, faintly worried. Or did he?

———

The two Spocks were eyeing each other with a mixture of wariness and disdain, like a man trying to fathom the operation of a trick mirror. Kirk was sure that his own expression was a good deal less judicious.

"Which of you," he demanded, "is the original?"

"I am, Captain," said both Spocks, in chorus.

"I was afraid you'd say that. Well, let's get one problem settled right now. Hereafter, I will address you," he pointed to the man on his left, "as Spock One, and you," he pointed to his right, "as Spock Two."

SPOCK MUST DIE!